Green

A novel

By Connie Williams

The author of *Emily's Blues*

 AWAP A Williams Acorn Publication
USA

GREEN is a work of fiction based on a true story. Any other references to real people in this work that resemble real persons, either living or dead; or to real places are intended only to give the work a setting in historical reality. Other names, characters, places and incidents either are the product of the author's imagination, used factiously, and their resemblance, if any, to real-life equals is entirely coincidental.

AWAP A Williams Acorn Publication
Correspondences emailed to: Cmae77@att.net

ISBN: 978-0-692-32371-7

Printed in the U.S.A.

Appreciation to: A visionary agent for causing me to lay some "fresh eyes" on the writing. And to "Uncle Buck" Donald L., Chet Art, Robin "Bird", Pam and Clint's care, Makeda-breathe in and Breathe out; Chernel V.; Mercedes T., Betty W. Special interview of "Toot" Coffey; "Tweet-tweet" Wynn, Aunt Mart, Jackie W; Mac the "brown Italian's always positive words; Chris' divine touch; and Carroll M's *l-o-n-g* discourse. Ben & Jen's V-Day sweets that helped me take a much needed break! Gina 'Baby-Girl's' kisses on my cheek, Gail-wind's love. Special thanks, also for Robbie's diligence and all Team members—they know who they are. This work would not be possible without them.

Dedicated to

My grand's Makeda, Zack, Rita, Clint Jr., Crystal,

Christopher, Marina, Dawn, Demetrius, Jerry Don,

Keef, Ishmael, and great grand's Shalom, Sinead,

Sade, Shiloh, Shanice Lynn who makes me think of

ice cream, Josiah, Donavon, Tamiah, Kamora, Axtel,

Joshe', Tatanne, Jordan, Jada, Destiny and 'Armad.

Especially in loving memory of Donna Lynne, Cory

and Connie Maria

1

There's an old saying in our family. *If you wash on New Year's Day you'll wash somebody right out of the family*. I forgot about it, and besides, I wasn't trying to remember one little bit of some old saying Mama believed in. So I washed a pair of socks, the green ones. Anyway, I couldn't find my white ones. I had on the blue socks. The dirty green ones were the only ones left; I suppose I had to wash the green ones even if it was New Year's Day because there was school the next day.

And then my granddaddy, poor old Daddy Claude died January 7, 1958, only one week after I washed the socks. My stomach tightens each time I think about it. I know if Mama learns about the socks, she will be some kind of upset and will blame me for Granddaddy not being here. She will say I washed Daddy Claude's life right out of him.

Soon everybody in Morris Town, North Carolina will know that Granddaddy is gone. Everything gets told, and it seems everybody comes to see and speak of the dead. But I can never tell what I did to Granddaddy; I want to make sure that no one ever finds out about me either. My stomach is turning over again; it feels like it did the day I had the fever and chills and Mama gave me the Black Draught.

Everything is moving along today I guess just like it is suppose to; everybody, including the men who come in the long black car, is speaking in almost a whisper, and Grandma's eyes are wet with tears at 4012 Fairley Avenue, until I cause this big uproar.

All I do is tiptoe over to Granddaddy's bed and lean down to kiss his forehead while I think nobody will see me, and Grandma nearly loses her mind.

My own grandma and my mama both turn into beasts in the matter of an instant—mean and ugly like I've never seen them before. Grandma's tears become hard like dry cornbread, the kind you can use for rocks.

"No Child!" Mama Allie opens her mouth wide; and screams from across the room with instantly stretched wet eyes, wildly waving both arms in the air; she runs and reaches for me at the same time. "What-in-the-world-you-doin? Lord Jesus!"

I stop right here in my tracks. I can't even move. And before she reaches me, Mama jumps in front of Grandma, and she grabs me by the arm real tight, snatching me from Granddaddy's bed. Grandma trips over her own feet making a big loud thump when she falls. She lands flat on the floor face down. Her eyeglasses fly across the room. I see her lying there.

As Mama yanks me from Granddaddy's bedside like she is pulling me from a blazing fire; she shakes me three or four times just about pulling my arm out of the socket. I feel like I might end up looking like my doll after my brother, Daniel, has gotten a hold of it and left it with missing arms. I don't know what is shaking more, my arm or Mama's head. In between shakes, I try to explain. "I just want to-to-say-goodbye. I-just—I want..."

In between shakes, Mama is yelling, "Now look-at what-you've done. You've got everybody-upset, and-you're in-the way." Her lips curl with anger; she stops shaking me but still holds my arm. "Girl, can't you see your poor ole' Granddaddy's dead? What's the matter with you? Now go on, Emilee, and get out of here!"

She lets go of my arm, and before I leave the room, I see Mama running over to Grandma who is still lying on the floor with everybody trying to pick her up. I hear Mama say to Grandma, "Mama, are you all right? Can you get up?"

It's like Grandma is waiting for Mama to be the one to help her up. Grandma finally sits up and she and Mama gave me a look that I understand that means, it is about as dangerous to stay in this room as it is to be on the streets of Morris Town—so leave now or else—else get your behind tore up.

I know there is no need to try to explain anything else at all. And crying will only get me into more trouble with Mama, so-I-don't-dare-do-it. I suck in my breath and hold in the tears that are trying to come out. And even though I try hard, I feel one wet drop trickle down my cheek anyway. I use the sleeve of my dress to wipe it off quickly. My leaving the room goes mostly unnoticed. As I leave, I look back and see all of them still crowded around Grandma who is finally up.

I feel like the disturbance inside is as bad as the one going on outside. The city of Morris Town is in huge turmoil. In this same month, January, a few days before Granddaddy died, the Ku Klux Klan motorcade rode down our street, where we live next door to Mama Allie and Granddaddy, on Fairley Avenue. That night my daddy came home from work and turned out all the lights in the house and told Mama, my sister Ruth, and my brother, Daniel, and me, "Stay down!" He meant for us to stay down on the floor to keep from getting hit by a brick thrown through the window, or something worse, getting shot and killed. We heard the thunderous roar of the motorcade and felt the "boom" of the Klansmen's shotguns through our whole bodies. Sparks from their gunfire sprayed the air while shouts and threats from hooded men echoed, "*We're gonna run dem niggers away from our town!*" I covered my head in fear; Daniel crouched in a corner.

Ruth's head popped up and down in an effort to steal a look outside. Ruth never passed up an opportunity to talk like grown folks. She later told us, what she had been thinking as she looked out of the window. 'If one of those MFs sets foot on that porch, I hope Daddy shoots "the sh--" out of him.' Mama and Daddy held on to each other on the floor beside the bed. Daddy crawled to a window and told us, "Dozens of motorcade carloads with Klansmen turned on First Street." It was later learned from the neighborhood news that they surrounded Dr. Phelps's house and burned a cross in the black doctor's yard.

The townspeople knew the Klan was calling for a hanging of two young black boys who were jailed for allegedly getting kissed by a white girl as the three of them played tag together one afternoon on the way home after school. Parents of the girl gathered with hooded whites and their shotguns. According to the news, white mothers fled their kitchens still wearing aprons and stormed the jailhouse ready to see that the young boys "met their maker." They said one mother yelled, "We'll teach him about kissing a white girl." And another one screamed, "Yeah, I'll kill him myself."

But I can't worry about what's going on with the town. I have my own trouble right in here. All I can think of is the man lying in the next room, Daddy Claude, who's dead because of me. I can't help wonder will those hooded men come for me; hang me for killing Granddaddy?

He's my grandfather, and they don't know, but I love him more than the green apple pie, my other Grandma Adessa makes, who lives on Bent Hill. And I **need** to say good-bye to him. For some people saying good-bye might be hard, but for me a good-bye can be easy when you love somebody, and they've been so good to you, and they've been close to you and loving you for all of your life. The thing about saying it now is if I don't say it now, it will be too late. When you love somebody the way I love Daddy Claude, you want to give him a good-bye kiss. But, ***they wouldn't even let me kiss Daddy Claude good-bye.***

After I leave the room, I think back to how Granddaddy looked lying on the old iron cot in Mama Allie's room (where he slept since he had his stroke) when those undertaker men came to take him in that long black car Mama Allie called the hearse. I can't stand to think of him in a hearse—a vehicle for a dead person which carries the coffin, "Whew!" He was so still.

It seems like all the objects in the whole house are still now. I think about how Mama, my grandma Mama Allie, and those men are so busy in the room where Granddaddy lies. But even they are trying to be still and move at the same time. My mama hardly moved her lips at all, and in her quietest voice ever, before she got mad at me for trying to kiss Daddy Claude, she told me to move out of the way and go to the kitchen with Aunt Florence. I wish my mind had told me to listen to her before I got her all upset. I suppose they're taking Granddaddy from the house to that place I heard Mama Allie call it the funeral parlor. That's why I had to kiss him now to whisper in his ear ***"I'm so, so, so, sorry Daddy Claude."***

The reason, I suppose, Mama told me to leave the room and go to the kitchen to wait with Aunt Florence is because it seems that Mama always thinks I'm nothing but a troublemaker. I suppose she thinks I'm too young to understand. But I know deep, deep down in my heart that Daddy Claude wouldn't want it this way.

On my way to the kitchen, I pass through Mama Allie's living room; I hear a reporter of the early news on the black and white television set say, today is January 7, 1958 and the Klansmen want RW, the NAACP President (RW is our thirty-five year old cousin, who vowed to save the two boys), and the Klan wants the vice president, Dr. Phelps to leave this town. They show pictures on the screen of the Freedom Riders in front of the courthouse led by RW, and Whites surrounding Negroes waving signs reading, "R W and your half-breed Negroes leave this town", while Negroes sing "We Shall Overcome" and carry signs that say "Justice for all." The reporter says it's not safe to be on the streets of Morris Town.

As I enter Mama Allie's dimly lit dining room on my way to the kitchen, the ghostly looking Old Woman in a dark photograph hanging on the wall, taunts me. ***"You washed that old man right out of the family! Didn't you***?" She causes me to stop instantly. Then Old Woman raises her eyes up to the cuckoo clock hanging on the wall above her photograph. I see the mechanical bird disappear behind a small door into the clock. When the cuckoo bird disappears, I see Witch, who only appears in the doorway of the clock to signal bad weather. But today she has come out of her cave to stand there—to help taunt me. The two of them, Old Woman and Witch cackle together their wretched disapproval and scorn. *"Ha-ha-ha-ha-ha-ha!"*

Suddenly the sun appears through the clouds outside and I feel the warmth on my face as it shines through curtains in the dining room. Old Woman and I watch as Witch darts into the clock inside her cave right before it strikes twelve o'clock. She is running from the sun, and I'm glad she's gone, but the force of the wind

7

from Witch's move into the clock causes me to land onto a chair all the way in the kitchen where I recall my mama's warning words.

It's not like I don't respect what Mama said about 'washing somebody out of the family.' I wasn't thinking about it. And I just can't see how someone can be in danger of dying by water unless he is caught in a flood or drowned in the creek or a river. So I thought Mama was just making a fuss over nothing, the way she always does, Daddy says, "running off at the mouth about stuff and 'hairy-assing' somebody, especially him, to death." And it's not that I don't respect dead people either.

One day I finally asked Grandma Allie's sister, Aunt Lil where her husband, Uncle Will was. She had a picture of him sitting on the mantle. I knew where my daddy was; I knew where Granddaddy and Mama's brother, Uncle Horace, were too. And it wasn't like I didn't know Uncle Will. One day he was there and the next week he was gone. Uncle Will was a black smith; I use to watch him shoe horses in his back yard. I watched him heat the horseshoe in a forge until it was red hot and use tongs to hold it to beat into shape on the anvil with a hammer then cool it in water before nailing it onto the horse's hoof. After he was gone, I kept expecting him to speak to me to tell me where he was—he never did. So when I asked her, Aunt Lil said, "The Lord has called him home to rest." Well, I had heard about the "Stairway to Heaven", in a song on the radio. And I must have been too little to remember when my great uncle died. So I asked, "You mean he walked up to heaven and went to bed?" "No, Baby, he died" she said. So, until now, I suppose that whenever people die, the Lord has called them home. I didn't want Granddaddy to get called home because of me.

The problem around here in Morris Town, North Carolina, is that people have too many old sayings about dead people, bad luck, hurting or killing somebody, and going to jail—about what I'm-***not***-suppose-to-do. Now it seems that Mama, Old Woman and Witch are all plotting together. They just keep making all these rules messing up my peace of mind.

I'm not supposed to point my finger at the graveyard or it will fall off. I hold my fingers down by my sides any time I'm around a graveyard, because I wouldn't want to have to show up at school in my teacher, Mrs. Faulkner's, class one day and not be able to write because I'm missing some of my fingers.

I'm not supposed to let the black cat cross my path, because it's bad luck. I ran around Mama Allie's house three times the other day just trying to get away from our neighbor, Miss Mae Lee's, old slow moving black cat that came sneaking from around the back yard of Grandma's house. I thought Witch had sent it to land me somewhere I didn't want to go. I finally looked back, and it had suddenly disappeared—disappeared into nowhere. That cat wasn't under the porch, and it wasn't in Mama Allie's woodshed—it wasn't anywhere to be found. All that week, I kept expecting that cat to come crawling out of Witch's cave. It didn't do that either.

I'm not supposed to step on the crack or I'll break Mama's back. I always had to remember to jump *over* the crack near the fireplace when we lived over there on Seaboard Street.

Jumping over wasn't always easy either, especially if I had any kind of speed behind me coming down the stairs like I usually did when I ran downstairs. Sometimes though, all I could do was rock back and forth from my heels to my toes, rotate my arms in the air, and hold in my breath and then jump. I held my breath 'cause if I let it go, I might surely jump right in the middle of that crack, and I would catch the blame for ruining Mama's back forever. Sometimes I would barely miss stepping on the crack. One old woman at church, Miss Tiphenia, is all bent over and can't walk without her walking cane. Now I wonder if one of her children wanted to get even with her for something she did to them by stepping on the crack, and now she is crippled forever.

I'm not supposed to get my feet swept or I'll go to jail. It sure looks like this one can't be stopped. With all of this buzzing around in my head all the time like honeybees swarming around a watermelon rind, it's no wonder that I couldn't remember what I wasn't supposed to do on New Year's Day, and that washing my green socks would wash, of all people, Granddaddy, out of the family. I don't remember anybody sweeping my feet; although it could have happened when Witch put a spell on me one day that caused me to fall asleep in a chair while Aunt Florence, Mama's youngest sister, swept the kitchen floor. Aunt Florence won't half pay attention to what she's doing anyway. I never knew anybody who will dry a dish and drop it onto the floor instead of into the sink because her mind is occupied with gazing out the window. So I know if she won't pay attention to what Mama Allie's calls her *good* dishes,

she certainly don't half pay attention to anything—
especially when somebody's feet might be in her way.

Granddaddy and his son, Uncle Horace could
never get along, and he was always talking about him
ending up going to the chain gang for something he'd
done, but it seems I will be the one going not him—that
is *if* they find out about what I've done to my poor,
poor, Granddaddy.

Here in the kitchen Aunt Florence doesn't speak
nor move; she doesn't even notice me at all. She stands
here by the dining room door holding her hands close
to her stomach, gazing across the room and out of the
window again, in deep thought. The look on her face is
like pain—hurting really, really, bad some place on her
body that she can't find. She's so still like Witch has
created a hole and planted her like a tree in that spot,
like she has put a spell over her.

As I sit here on one of Grandma's old dining
room chairs by the warm kitchen stove, I can smell
wood burning. And I smell the coffee that was made
for breakfast this morning that still sits on the stove in
Grandma's silver colored, aluminum coffeepot. I still
have a scar on my hand from a burn, when I tried to
pour Mama Allie a cup of coffee one day. Grandma
must have not had time to take the pot off the stove
before Daddy Claude died.
I can hear murmuring voices from the bedroom
that float down through the living room and the dining
room into the kitchen. I can hear the front door screen
slam---blam! Then everybody except Aunt Florence and
me are outside. I run and open the back door to look

through the screen. I can hear them talking in low voices. I want to see if Daddy Claude is gone—if they have taken him away in that big car.

The latch on the door is located high up on the screen, and it's too tight and difficult to open. So I press my face against the screen and watch. I see Grandma Allie standing in the yard near the old black wash pot among a group of people. Her body is as straight as a ladder with bumps. The wind is blowing hard. If there were leaves on the trees, they would be flapping in the cold rush of the air. Mama, Mama Allie, Aunt Lil and two ladies from across the street, her friends, Miss Anna Lee and Miss Burla's skirt tails dance with the wind as they pull their coats tight to keep from shivering. They stand and talk quietly.

Their heads are held low; their lips flour white and dry. Their eyes look sad, like someone has taken a dark pencil and drawn lines around them. Mama Allie looks thin like the wind could scoop her up and blow her like the dust. I wish my Mama would put her arm around Grandma to help hold her down. I don't want her to get blown down by the wind.

I hear Miss Anna Lee say to Grandma, "He sure was a good man. I'm glad he didn't suffer. You say he died in his sleep?" She shakes her head and pats Mama Allie on the back. "If you need anything, Sugar, you just let me know."

The long hearse starts up, backs out of Mama Allie's front yard, pulls off, and turns the corner up Blyer Street. And right behind it, Mr. Albert pulls up in his yellow and black taxicab with the motor in the car still running while Mama and her mother climb into the back seat and close the car door. Then I see the taxi pull off with two jerks of the car and two jerks of Mr. Albert's head and two jerks of Mama and Mama Allie's heads like three birds sitting on a limb.

I keep my face pressed against the screen and watch as long as I can until I can't see it anymore, the black car, or the taxicab. As I stand at the screen door thinking real hard and turning what happened over and over in my mind and wondering how things got so messed up, a strange feeling starts to well up in my head and my heart—a feeling I can't explain that makes me feel hot all over. This feeling comes over me quickly. My heart shrinks, and these actions run through my memory.

It had rained a good, long rain and our yard was full of black mud puddles that I just couldn't help splashing in most of Sunday afternoon. I was having plenty of fun and forgot about suppertime. Mama called me in to eat. The wet mud was all I could smell, so I didn't even get a whiff of that sweet potato pie my daddy made us for supper. Mama said I was plenty dirty too, especially my socks. They had black mud from the yard on them from top to bottom. Mama said that I looked like a mud hog, too dirty to eat supper looking like that, and to change my clothes. I changed my pants; I remember taking off the green socks and putting on the blue ones.

Right after I ate my pie I left the table to find my other socks. I looked everywhere, but I couldn't even find the white ones. Although it was New Year's Day, I had to wash the green ones to have a clean pair for school.

The screen marks are lined on my face from pressing against it just like the guilt pressed there. If my grandma takes a good look at me, I surely know she will see the guilt pressed there. I see Aunt Lil, Miss Burla and Miss Anna Lee walk from the front yard back to the house. They come inside. My stomach feels so tight, and I feel so weak I have to sit down again in the chair beside the stove. The heat from the stove feels like it is going through my whole body. My arms, feet and legs tingle, especially my stomach. It helps me. I don't feel so weak now like I can't get my breath.

I suppose her spell is broken; Aunt Florence finally moves as if she suddenly comes back to life. She walks over and unlatches the screen door. She speaks to me. "Emilee, I'm going up front. You need to go on down the path to home." She turns to go up to the living room to be with the others and leaves me sitting here.

I walked down that same path with my Uncle Horace and then we walked to Hog Pen Hill to slop my granddaddy's two hogs inside the pen. I remember after Daddy Claude had a stroke and before the Klan rode through and the whole town was in trouble with RW and the Freedom Riders, it was safe to be on the streets. Daddy Claude said the hogs had to be fed every afternoon if we wanted to fatten them up to have one for Thanksgiving and Christmas dinner. So he said we didn't have a whole lot of time.

My uncle wasn't too fond of slopping the hogs and much less fond of taking me along with him. But Daddy Claude would just make him take me with him anyway. "Catch Emilee by the hand and take her with you when you go down to the hog pen today." He would say.

Uncle Horace would gather the slop and reach for me with one hand, swinging the bucket with the other. He would hold my hand so tight and walk so fast with his long legs; I sometimes almost had to run just to keep up with him. I kept up though. I wanted to tell Granddaddy that I didn't want to go, but he was counting on me. I knew he wanted me to look after Uncle Horace.

I remember Uncle Horace wore his old coveralls with one strap unbuttoned and hanging. It would be hot outside, and he would be "three sheets in the wind" as Mama said. It seemed that this funny smell would be coming from his skin, and beads of water dripped off his face down into his shirt. So I guess he wore his pants that way to stay cool. His unbuttoned strap would slap against his back, slap-walk-slap-walk-slap-walk. When he fed the hogs, he would sling slop everywhere and talk to himself about Granddaddy. And when the bucket was empty, he found his favorite sitting hole under the pine needle tree where he always sat when he was down at the pen.

It was just plain sad to see him that way. He looked so lonesome sitting there. He pulled out his bottle of Seagram's Seven, I saw written on the bottle that he hid from Granddaddy and gulped in a mouth full that puffed out his jaws until he swallowed it. I could always tell whenever he was up to something. The funny smell wasn't the only thing that gave him away.

15

On the way to the pen, he would make funny noises and make believe he heard something in the bushes. It was like, without words, he was saying I had better not tell Granddaddy about what he was doing, or that thing we heard out there was sure to come to get me when I went to bed. I was always sorry when he finished feeding the hogs and went to sit under the pine tree because he didn't talk anymore about anything to himself or me. Therefore, I had nothing to take my mind off being there. I had nothing to take my mind off the scary stuff at the old house on Seaboard Street-- the mangy old mules across the alley that Uncle Horace said would get me if they got loose. Nor the stuff now-- the dreaded, dark photograph of Woman in Mama Allie's dining room that Aunt Florence is really, really scared of because she says it's cursed, Witch and her magical powers, nor the cracking sounds of the back room where Maw, Mama Allie's mother slept before she died. So, I would skip around and around the pen playing and singing, *"I lost my handkerchief yesterday and found it today. And it was full of buttermilk and so I dashed it away, away- away-away."*

I just couldn't understand why Uncle Horace was so mad at Granddaddy all of the time, though, and why he was so pitiful himself. Granddaddy just kept on warning him if he didn't stop his ways, he would end up in a whole lot of trouble like the chain gang. Mama said that it was an awful place where people who broke the law and did a crime and were locked up, wore chains shackled around the ankles "bust" rocks and that I sure wouldn't want to go there. I asked her why were they "busting" rocks. She told me to stop asking her so many "dat-blame" questions because she was too busy to talk anymore. I couldn't ask Daddy Claude he had had a stroke. I sure wish Mama could have told me more about it; that way I would not have to struggle with my own imagination about it. I intended to look it up in the encyclopedia.

Anyway, I heard Uncle Horace's wife, Aunt Glenice try her best to talk some sense into him. "You ought to be ashamed of yourself. You got a good daddy, his wife told him. You ought to be glad to help him with whatever you can. You know that man is sick. If he wasn't he would do it all, EVERYTHING, himself."

Uncle Horace complained, "That man never did much for anybody but himself. He *never* did anything for me while he was well."

"That's your father you're talking about, Horace," I remember Glenice shot back.

This made Uncle Horace so mad he started to tremble and foam at the mouth like our dog Frock, when he was on to some stranger. He breathed hard and spread the corners of his mouth together like he was about to bite. His color changed from brown, to dark brown.

Aunt Glenice moved to the other side of the room out of his reach. "You got a good daddy, Horace." She still insisted.

Uncle Horace whirled around as if he was my red spinning top then reeled across the room. He stood in front of his wife. "Yeah, I got a good daddy all right. It's awfully funny that you didn't think he was so good when I came home from the Army and he wouldn't even feed you and the children. He was eating plenty high on the hog, and you all were starving—all of you. Times were really hard. You know how our poor little girl, Clarice, got so sick from hunger. Girl, you know that yourself. When you told me you got credit at Reverend Isenhour's store, I thanked the Lord. If it hadn't been for that good white man, I don't know what we would have done. I was embarrassed, Glenie, because I couldn't feed and take care of my family. And, my own daddy wouldn't help me. He didn't give a dime about what happen to us. And too, what hurt me doubly bad was that he wouldn't let my own mama help us either. He knew I needed money to look for a job. And now he thinks we should all fall at his feet."

Uncle Horace looked a way that I had never seen him before—like he was truly hurting--the way he looked sitting under the tree. He looked like a little sad puppy, one that's been left behind by the whole family.

He told Aunt Glenice, "That just tore me up inside girl. Now you know that. He sat there on his fat butt and told me, those are your children, and you take care of them. I haven't had one baby by Glenice." I saw Uncle Horace squeezed both of his fists, raised them up into the air. "That was the one time I was tempted to hit my own father. I wanted to leave his house so bad, but where was I going to go and take you and the kids? So we had to stay in his house."

I remember hearing every word that Uncle Horace said that day, and Aunt Glenice could see that how Uncle Horace felt about Daddy Claude was making my eyes fill with tears. She knew how I felt about my granddaddy too. So I remember she leaned down toward me and I could feel her warm breath on my face, and I got a whiff of the cigarette she was smoking too.

She whispered, "Don't you pay your crazy Uncle no mind. After all, his daddy was kind enough to put a roof over our heads the whole time your uncle was in the Army. After all, if it hadn't been for him, we would have had no place to stay. At least that was something. The Lord knows we sure couldn't have stayed with my family." She stood and took her hand and held my face close to her body and squeezed my shoulder two or three times. I pressed my face against the side of her long slim body as she put her arm around me. She was thin but she felt strong.

My thoughts leave Granddaddy being dead and that I caused it. All I can think of now is what I remember my uncle saying and that he didn't think Granddaddy was a nice man. It is hard to think that Daddy Claude wouldn't help his own grandchildren when they needed him. That would be awful.

This kind of thinking was making me feel strange, and I didn't like it much at all. What I heard Miss Anna Lee say when she was standing in the yard repeatedly popped back into my mind. I remember her saying to Grandma, "You had a good husband, Sugar. Most women round here in Morris Town sure would like to have a good man like he was. He sure was good to you." So how could what Uncle Horace said be true?

I know myself that a good man like my grandfather would love his grandchildren and let them help themselves at his table for whatever they wanted, especially when he had so much for himself.

My mind drifts back to my granddaddy and my whole predicament when I hear Aunt Florence coming back to the kitchen.

"You're still sitting here, Emilee? I thought I told you to go on home." I don't put up any fuss; I get up. Aunt Florence opens the door where she had unlatched the back screen and turns and walks away. I do exactly as she tells me to do. I walk out of the door down the steps and down the path to home.

<u>2</u>

The strange feeling wells up in my head and my heart again. I feel hot and cold all over, and it makes me feel so sad that I want to cry. I wish I didn't feel so awful. It's the middle of the afternoon, and I'll be the only one home right now, so I can go ahead and cry and no one will see me. I can go ahead and find my socks too, and bury them in the back yard before anybody finds out. I run inside the house to my room to search for them. When I find them, I'll bury them just like they're going to bury Granddaddy. I sit down to think; my head feels just so, so heavy, heavy with guilt, heavy with shame, heavy with worry—I have to hold it up with my hands cuffed underneath my chin.

What I can't understand is I don't know why Mama didn't give me some new socks for Christmas, so I would have more than three pairs. That's why I had to wash the green ones in the first place. And now of all things, Mama bought new socks for me and the green ones have disappeared just like Miss Mae Lee's black cat that I still haven't seen. I can't find them anywhere. I wanted to tell Mama it's too late for new socks now. Granddaddy is already dead.

Everything would be fine if Mama had given me new socks instead of that ugly brown snowsuit she bought me, which no one else has, which I hate, and which makes me look like the silliest fifth grader in the whole school—the whole world. It's a wonder I haven't gotten beat up by old bad Billie Woods, the school bully, for wearing it. He is always pounding one of his fists into his hand and threatening to beat somebody up. I saw him light into a schoolmate, Odell Little, one day on the school yard, with both fists and feet flying then finally, stumbling, falling backwards and both of them rolling over the ground all because of a Baby Ruth candy bar. When our teacher, Mrs. Faulkner, pulled them apart, they both just laughed about it; afterwards the principal, Mr. Charles, sent them home for the rest of the day.

Anyway, on weekdays at school, the boys make me be the Indian when we play cowboys and Indians during recess. Vettie, my best friend, who lives across the street from me, always gets to play the girl in danger. She gets saved by the cowboys because she's pretty with two long braids that hang down to her shoulders, and she wears dresses to school. James, who has dimples and curly hair and who happens to be the cutest and the smartest boy in the fifth grade, is the one that always says, "Let Emilee be the Indian." And they all, he, his friend Bert, a well-dressed and shiny looking boy my same age; he lives across the tracks, and Vettie band together to choose me. So I have to run away from them all over the school yard as they chased after me. They chase me past the school steps; pass the school entrance, almost out of breath, over to the end of the yard, across from where Granddaddy often sent me to Mr. Figures' neighborhood corner store. Then I'm chased back past the steps again to the other end of the yard across from Mama Allie's and Vettie's house; sometimes, pausing just enough to see how much they were gaining on me. They chased me with my heart beating hard in my chest within an inch of my life. And I always ended up getting caught on my way back to the steps knowing that they could have caught up with me long before, but they wanted to have what was a good time for them—but not for me.

Finally, when they caught up with me, then each cowboy drew his two guns to shoot me dead with all four. Twirling their guns backwards into holsters like the Lone Ranger, they pretended to do what they say the white man did to the Indian on Television when he caught him. Sometimes I felt if I didn't run fast enough, they would kill me **for sure**. I wish, just once, I could play the pretty girl that gets saved by the cowboys. But how can I wearing that big brown snowsuit? Then after I'm dead, they leave me lying there to pick my own self up. They take Vettie by the hand and walk her up the school steps of Winchester School exchanging smiles. I know if I wore a dress and ribbons more often like Vettie, it would be different. James would smile at me.

My mama just doesn't know what a hard time she causes me to have. I know I can't ever tell her either; she won't believe me—not a word I say.

Before I have a chance to do what I planned, my daddy comes home from work. Just as I am about to look into the last chifforobe drawer, I hear him come in the front door. My heart stops because the first thing he will do if he doesn't see Mama in the kitchen, is come to the back of the house where my sister Ruth's and my bedroom is to see whose home.

"Anybody home?" I hear him call. He doesn't know about Granddaddy. He walks to my room, and I quickly put all of the clothes back into the drawer before he catches me. I finish just in time before he enters the door. "Emilee, where's your mama?"

I look up, trying to swallow to get the lump out of my throat and trying to keep him from seeing my guilt, and I start to tell him about Granddaddy and that Mama is up the path at Mama Allie's house.

After I tell Daddy about Granddaddy, he goes to the bathroom to wash his face and hands. Then he goes to the bedroom to take off his work shoes. He always takes off the shoes he wore to work because they have tacks in the bottom of them from working in the upholstery shop all day, and they stick his feet. He puts on another pair, and he then leaves the house and goes right up the path to be with Mama and Mama Allie. He didn't turn on the television like he's been doing to see the news and what the news people are saying about the Negroes and the Whites. He didn't even go to his old, as Mama says, 'home-away-from-home, his "shot gun" upholstery shop: one window, a door—one way in and one way out', the upholstery shop he built in the back yard, although he has a sofa to finish for a white man, Mr. Michael by next Saturday.

As soon as I find those socks, and that might be harder now that I have run out of places to look, and as soon as my brother, Daniel, comes home, after supper, I'll find a case knife in the kitchen and get Daniel to help me pull some of those tacks out of Daddy's shoes so they won't stick him tomorrow when he goes to work. I know Daniel will want to add the large headed tacks to the collection he's saving to make taps with bottle caps that he tacks onto his shoe heels, to make them sound like a tap dancer's shoes when he walks.

I look under the beds for the third time to see if I missed anything, but I didn't. The only things under the bed are what I saw the first time—a box with a pair of Ruth's old sneakers and dust. I look behind the table by the door; I look behind the old sofa that Daddy put in our room and said he would cover over a month ago. And I still can't find my socks. Anyway, I'm exhausted, hungry and just plain want to give up for now. I haven't even done my homework either. And I don't know how I can, being this worried about my socks and about Granddaddy.

"Oh no, Daniel is already home." I can hear him in the kitchen lifting the lids off the pots on the stove. So I will just have to put everything on hold for now because I know my brother. If he gets any idea that something is going on, he won't let me rest until he needles every bit of it out of me. My sister Ruth comes home from basketball practice too.

With Mama and Daddy both up the path at Mama Allie's, I wait and listen to hear my sister and brother make small talk about everybody's whereabouts. Then I rush out of the bedroom to the kitchen where they are to break the news about Granddaddy's death and that I saw him dead on his cot in the room before the men took him away.

Ruth uses her grown up thirteen-year-old talk. She wants to know how long after Granddaddy passed was the body taken away before she came home. Was the police called? Did the neighbors know? What did they say and do? She asks questions that send a chill over me. I shake myself to spill out responses like shaking coins that spill out of a piggy bank. It is difficult, but I do my best not to let on about the murder. **Murder**, did I say murder? I tell myself, a person can get time on the chain gang for killing someone. Just think, I'll have to wear chains around my ankles and work at the railroad busting rocks in the hot sun all day. When Granddaddy talked about someone going to that awful place, he had no idea that it might be *me*. The thought feels like cold burning my temples now—as if I'd drank down an ice cold glass of water, the way it feels when I drink it too fast. What in the world am I going to do? How can I stay calm knowing what I know?

Ruth walks to the back of the house. I follow her because today I don't want to act any differently than any other day; and our brother follows me. We waddle through Mama and Daddy's room to our bedroom like three ducks one after the other. My brother sits on the edge of my bed, and I stand holding on to the bedpost. My sister removes her shoes and socks and is just about to pull her shirt over her head when she tells Daniel to leave the room. He slides down off the bed and runs from the room without a word; knowing Daniel, he's probably going to work on his taps made of bottle caps before going out to play.

I know it won't be too long before my sister expects me to leave the room too. I gladly make my exit. I ease out without having her ask me. Besides, I had bundled the clothes up in her drawer and had thrown them back in when Daddy came home. I didn't have a chance to think of an explanation. And I know she would want one or she would tell Mama on me.

Just as I cross into Mama and Daddy's room, my sister asks something that I cannot hear, and I stop cold in my path waiting for her to ask what happened to her clothes, and she repeats her words. I hear her say, "Did you cook anything?"

With relief, I answer her, "No. But I'll fry some potatoes and bologna and open some green peas." I move swiftly to the kitchen to cook. I need something to take my mind off my trouble and Daddy Claude.

It's not often, but my sister seems to be in a good mood, like the way everything goes as I cook. I quietly move about the kitchen making dinner, trying my best to keep my mind on the cooking and not the death. I watch Mama all of the time in the kitchen when she's cooking. I can cook a lot of stuff. I can't make Daddy's favorite dish, Hungarian Goulash, but I can make biscuits, grits, and eggs. I haven't tried to fry a chicken. Mama is afraid I might burn myself real bad with the hot grease, but I sure do know how to fry potatoes and bologna 'cause it doesn't take as long to cook and it doesn't take as much grease as it does to fry a chicken. Mama said she don't care too much for eating fried chicken anyway. She says she's had to wring too many chicken necks and pluck too many chicken feathers in her lifetime when she and Aunt Lil killed chickens for the local food store. So she seldom ever wants to eat one. So we don't have chicken that much.

I do everything the way Mama showed me. When everything is ready, I put it in bowls and place it carefully in the middle of the table with three plates, forks, and spoons surrounding them.

"Dinner's ready." I call. Both Ruth and Daniel move quickly to the table and sit down to eat as quietly as a baby lying on cotton. I suppose because Daddy Claude's death hangs in the air over our heads and in our thoughts. I'm sure it hangs in my thoughts more than anyone of the other two because it is my fault. He deserves the quiet respect that I am sure to give him, but I am surprised at Ruth's actions. She usually cuts up on anything and everything.

Ruth says the grace to bless the food. "Lord we thank you for this food. Amen." While she prays for the food, I sneak in a prayer for help to find my green socks. I sure hope that the Lord hears me. Whenever I pray for something real important, I usually get an answer and right away too. I prayed for an 'A' on my math test, and I prayed that Daddy Claude would walk again after his stroke. Both times the Lord answered me. I hope He'll hear me this time too. I sure do need Him.

We eat our food in loud silence. The sounds are of the forks on the plates as my brother scoops the last of the peas with his fingers to eat them and my sister chews with her lips curled. From time to time, our eyes meet in unison only to drop our heads immediately as we are in deep thought.

As I sit here, I wonder. My mind is floating in a sea of thoughts when my sister's words come up out of nowhere like something huge, breaking open the water. She says, "By Tuesday we should know if Daddy Claude's funeral will most likely be on Friday."

I feel relief that our silence is broken because it is about to get the best of me. It is as though my thoughts have hands, and they're trying to push the words right out of my mouth. One more minute and no telling what I might tell on myself.

As she eats, Ruth dabs the corner of her mouth with her fingers, and continues to talk as she tears a slice of bologna in half and begins to stuff it into her mouth. I watch her eat. She chews and swallows. "I just knew he wasn't going to live much longer after his stroke." As she sits here talking grown up, I can see she bears what some of the grown folks call a striking resemblance to Mama. She speaks the way Mama speaks, and she closes her mouth clenching her teeth the way Mama does. And her chin is Mama's chin too. She has what people say is Mama's keen fine features and Mama's beauty too. There is no question about it. No wonder Mama loves her the way she does.

My mind drifts back out into the sea of thoughts again, and I wonder what should I wear to my grandfather's funeral? I suppose my Grandma will be dressed in all black. But I know I can't wear black because I don't even own a black dress. I have black shoes that I got for Christmas that I can still wear but no black dress. Knowing Mama, she might try to make me wear that brown snowsuit, especially if it's real cold. I have a navy blue dress with a white music note on the front of it that Mama made for me last year when I sang at school on stage in the music recital. I haven't grown much since last year so I can still wear it. But it's made of nylon. I'll freeze in that. It's the beginning of January, and cold most of the time. And a lot of the time there's frost on the ground, like now.

Daniel finishes his dinner and breaks into my thoughts when he asks for more Kool-Aid. I hand him the plastic pitcher and he pours his glass half full of red cherry, and takes it with him when he leaves the table, I suppose he's anxious to work on his tap shoes with the bottle caps again.

It's strange now that I remember, it was cold when our little baby sister, Sarah, died three years ago. I was eight, and she was only twenty-three days old. I remember that morning, as clearly as if it was yesterday. Mama screamed, and I flew from the bed into her room to see what was wrong. Mama cried, "Sarah's not breathing!" And surly enough she wasn't. She looked like one of my dolls lying there all still—eyes closed. She was already kind of purple and blue looking. At least her lips were. I held her for a short while, and then Mama took her from me. My mama cried so hard. She cried loud gulping sounds. I thought she was never going to stop especially after the funeral at the graveyard when they put that little box that Sarah was in into the ground. Daddy was trying to hold Mama up to keep her from falling down. She was so weak from all that sobbing. It wasn't January, it was spring, but it was so cold that we had to wear our coats.

Now that I think about my little sister who died, it didn't bother me one bit to hold her while she was dead, and it didn't give me any nightmares either. They all said when I was little that I used to cry a lot at night. We lived over there on Seaboard Street in that big house with our grandparents, Uncle Horace, his wife and three children, where Ruth, Daniel, and Uncle Horace's children and I were all born. That old house had a long stairway that curved down into the living room by a dusty and old gray, ashy fireplace, the one I had to jump over to keep from breaking Mama's back. Uncle Horace was always telling us some story to "scare us into being good" as he would say. Our house was across the alley from Mr. Hoyle Hoffman's house, and he owned those two old mangy-looking mules, the local hamburger joint, as Mama Allie called it, and the ice cream, candy and soda pop store down the street on Winchester.

When I cried at night, it wasn't because Uncle Horace had told his favorite story to all of us about wartimes or the local ax murder, which happened to be true and the whole town happened to know all about it, he said. And the woman, according to Uncle Horace, walked around at night looking for her head that was chopped off by the man who was her lover and who lived next door to my grandmother. He stole Mama Allie's ax and used it to cut off the woman's head, and then he threw the ax into the ditch down the road, or the story about the mules jumping the fence to come and get me.

I cried so I would be allowed to stay up with Mama Allie, and she would let me play outside under the Chinaberry tree, watch the fireflies or fly my June bug, when the weather was warm. My teacher, Mrs. Faulkner says a June bug is a phyllophaga beetle.
Seems to me, the grown folks should have figured that one out, since I never cried at night during the winter. What bothers me the most though is that most of the people around here in Morris Town, North Carolina, at least the ones I know are afraid of dead people. And for the life of me, I just can't see why. What can a dead person do to you? Shoot! The one's I'm afraid of are alive—like Mama, who would whip me but good if she knew how I feel and the real reason I used to cry at night. And she will *kill* me for sure if she ever finds out about those socks and what I've done to my poor Granddaddy.

Anyway, I *was* just a little bit scared of Uncle Horace's stories too, especially when he had us gather around him as he told about: being in the war, shooting guns, dodging bullets, blood dripping and crawling out of foxholes from dead bodies with bulging eyes. But I could sleep at night because he knew that I knew all about him and about that bottle he carried with him down to Hog Pen Hill. And I knew about the books he carried with the pictures of those ladies wearing all that frilly stuff, and some not wearing anything at all that he looked at while he sat there under the pine needle tree that I am sure Aunt Glenice didn't know anything about.

And I knew about the things he would say about Granddaddy too.

One night I had had another one of my crying fits, and Mama Allie was taking her own sweet time about coming to rescue me; I had begun to get worried not to mention how tired I was from crying. I would cry a little while and listen a little while. There was a loud bumping sound on the roof, and Uncle Horace later came in and said that, if I didn't stop crying those mules were surely going to be after me. I finally heard Mama Allie at the bottom of the stairs, and she called up to me. "Come on down-stairs, baby." I was so little then, that Grandma had tied a string to the light switch that hung low enough so I could reach up and turn on the light. At the top of the stairs, just before turning on the light, I could see by the moonlight shining into the window a tall thing stood there with an old dark blanket over it and a wire clothes hanger on its head. Till this day, I know that was nobody but old Uncle Horace on that step. As my grandma says, I know that as good as I know my name.

Uncle Horace is still up to his same old tricks because after he moved his family, and we moved from Seaboard Street to Fairley, where we live now, I knew where he got his bottles from, too, that he carried to the Hog Pen Hill. He took them from Granddaddy's hiding place behind the baseboard in the dining room that led to the kitchen. I saw him go and get one when Granddaddy was in the bathroom. It took Daddy Claude a long time to move from one room to another after his stroke. He would have to pull himself up by handles that Mama Allie had nailed to the walls. So, my uncle had all the time he needed to take what he wanted. I was just about to go into the dining room; Uncle Horace must have not seen me at all. He put the bottle in his pocket and pushed the nails back in place and rushed to the kitchen and out the back door.

I couldn't tell on my uncle because I had secrets of my own. That hiding place was the storage for Daddy Claude's and Mama Allie's private store that they had in the dining room, to where their customers from the mills, the bakery, and the railroad came, still wearing their work clothes at the end of the day to buy Seagram's Seven.

They gulped down from little crystal glasses before going home in the evening. They would give me the pretty, shiny seal with the red ribbon that was tied and hanging around the neck of the bottle.

Granddaddy made a whole bunch of money from selling "shots" or Seagram's Seven in crystal shot glasses too. The reason I know is because he let me climb up into a chair on my knees to count the money that he kept in his money pouch. I was a good counter. I would stack all the ones in even stacks and all the fives in even stacks all the tens in even stacks and all the twenties in even stacks. I did the same thing for the change, too. I would stack the pennies, the nickels, the dimes, the quarters and the fifty-cent pieces in stacks, and then I would count everything. While I counted I would first try to slip a dollar into my own pocket when Granddaddy wasn't looking, so I could buy something good to eat from Mangums store. But Aunt Florence was always standing around somewhere paying attention to everything I did when I was counting

Granddaddy's money. The stuff she should have been careful about like Mama Allie's good dishes and sweeping somebody's feet, made no difference to her at all. So every time I slid a dollar into my pocket, she made sure she went into my pocket and put it right back on the table. She never told on me, but she made sure I left there the same way I came, with my pockets empty.

That same private store brought the sheriff to their house one day. I thought those men in brown and white were looking for Uncle Horace for something he had done, since Daddy Claude had talked so much about something bad happening to him and all. But they were trying to find that hiding place where Granddaddy kept his bottles. And they just about tore the place up. Mama Allie said that big red sheriff from downtown was determined to come up with something. He kept going back and looking in the same places. The more he looked, the redder he got. The redder he got, the more he looked. Finally, frustrated, he gave up and left because he couldn't find anything. The next day, Mama Allie said she got up "bright and early" to walk up the street to Mangum's store to buy a local Morris Town Newspaper so she and Daddy Claude could read it and find out about whom the sheriff had caught during the raid.

It was fine and perfectly cool with me when they decided to close the store, since it almost got me in big trouble. I had seen the customers drink from the crystal glasses, and I had seen Uncle Horace gulp down a drink from his bottle—smack his lips and say "Hah" like it tasted so good, just like good old ice tea, the kind

Mama makes with plenty of sugar in it. So one day I thought I would sneak a drink of that good stuff as soon as Mama Allie turned her back. The open bottle and the pretty, little crystal glass seemed to be calling my name. I grabbed it, poured the glass full of whiskey, and sat the bottle down. My hand was shaking so I almost spilled it onto the floor. I dashed the stuff, the whole glass, into my mouth quickly, just like Uncle Horace and an afternoon customer. In my mind, I was planning to gulp it down and say "Hah!" just like Uncle Horace.

Old Woman in the photograph hanging on the wall eyed me; she asked, *What did you do that for?* Witch, above her inside the cuckoo clock was inside her cave. I needed her magical powers to whirl me home because I surely didn't know what I was getting myself into, and I certainly couldn't answer Old Woman's question. I couldn't move; it was burning my whole mouth, my tongue; I couldn't swallow, and Mama Allie was coming around the corner back into the room, and there was no place to spit the stuff out either. I did the only thing I could do. I headed for the back door and ran right into Aunt Florence with her arms full bringing in some firewood. She took me by surprise and I swallowed a mouthful of Seagram's Seven. Now why anybody would want to drink that burning, nasty stuff is beyond what I know.

After that swallow, my head started to spin and my stomach was cutting flips like one of Daddy's flapjacks he tossed into the air on Sunday morning when he made us breakfast. I wanted to get on my knees and crawl, which is exactly what I had to do to get down the path to home. I know one thing to be true for sure. If I was on the deathbed, and Seagram's Seven was the only thing that would make me well, I would just have to die and be buried. Come to think of it, I suppose I do believe in some of this superstitious stuff a little bit after all because I keep hoping for Witch's help. I suppose Mama sure would be happy.

Dinner is over, and with a very tired mind, I get up from the table, clear it and start to run some water in the kitchen sink to wash the dishes before Mama and Daddy come home.

Ruth must still be feeling all right because she brings the bowls of food and puts them on the stove. We both move about the kitchen working together like two mechanical parts in motion. She walks over, turns on the radio and WMAP is playing "Around the World" by Patty Page, and we both start to sing in harmony while we clean the kitchen. But I know this togetherness will all change as soon as she finds her clothes messed up in the chifforobe drawer. She'll be as mad as Mama Allie's old red hen when it runs from under the house to tear after somebody playing with a Hula-Hoop. I've never seen a hen so set against Hula-Hoops in my life. Anyway, Ruth and I will be back to enemies as usual. All this harmony stuff will all be over.

So we finish up the kitchen; and I'm sweeping the floor when Mama, Daddy and Uncle Horace come in. My daddy has the most serious look on his face that I would believe his father has died. The skin is folded on his forehead with deep lines. All three of them come straight to the kitchen. Daddy sits at the kitchen table, and Mama goes to the stove to warm the meal.

Uncle Horace stands there by the table for a while and then he says, "I guess I'd better be getting on home to Glenice and *them* chaps."

Daddy asks him, "Stay a while and have a bite to eat."

Uncle Horace looks at his watch and checks the time. He seems to be pondering whether to take Daddy up on his offer. After he checks the time, he rubs his large hands on his pants several times like they're wet and he's trying to dry them. He says, "Um nine thirty. Supper smells good, but Glenie will be wondering about me after a while. So, I'd better get on home and get ready to meet the man in the morning. I'll be by here after work tomorrow to see if I can help you out with anything. If you need me before that, you know where I'll be, down there at the railroad station. I'm gone." He leaves, and we hear him crank up the motor of his motorcycle, and he takes off. I listen until I don't hear it anymore.

Their coming home reminds me of all the events that have gone on all over again. If anybody had asked me if this washing somebody out of the family stuff was for real, I would have wondered if they were making any good sense at all. Maybe I need to pay more attention to it. It's like someone holds a mirror up that shows me wringing out the wet socks and then poor old Daddy Claude lying on the cot in his room dead as dirt. Although it is late, I leave Mama and Daddy in the kitchen and go to start work on my spelling words, just in case I go to school tomorrow. We're up to the 'N.'

<u>3</u>

Today is Friday, Daddy Claude's funeral is at two; Mama says at Friendship Baptist Church. She said for us to be dressed and ready to leave the house by twelve thirty. Grier's Funeral Home sends the long black car. This time it comes to Mama Allie's front door to pick all of us up. Mama Allie, Mama and Daddy ride in the front seat with the driver who is long and thin and wearing the blackest, shiniest suit, that I have ever seen. It's so black that he seems to be a part of the dark seat he's sitting in. Most of us are all dressed in black except for Nerissa, our cousin who has come from New York with her mother, Mama's oldest sister, Odessa, and me. I wear a dark blue skirt and starched white blouse; Nerissa wears grey.

I ride in the middle with Aunt Florence, Uncle Horace and Aunt Glenice. My sister Ruth and brother Daniel sit in the back seat with our aunt Odessa, with Nerissa. Everybody is quiet for the occasion. The thoughts of seeing Granddaddy for one last time is on my mind. When the car starts up, Ruth starts up too, to break the quietness; she makes knock-knock jokes with Nerissa, keeps giggling while Aunt Odessa keeps putting her finger up to her lips—keeps telling her "S h-h-h-h." trying to shush her.

The ride in the long black car did not need to leave the familiar trails of Morris Town and the boundaries of our Colored neighborhoods, where we live, the funeral parlor, the church and the cemetery. As we roll steadily along I think, these streets show no sign of the city's on-going trouble, living under lynch laws: midnight shootings, the beatings of blacks on the streets, according to the TV, sometimes these awful incidents take place right in the courthouse square. Throwing of rocks and bottles at homes in black neighborhoods, gunshots, the slaying of Blacks, the drowning in water holes of young children, as I heard Mama say, children my own age just hoping for a summer swim. The magnitude of what's going on, as I gaze out the car window, is far beyond my imagination—I think if someone asks me, I wouldn't know, but I know it's locked into the hearts of my parents and grandparents. Those in the community know all of them.

The clock in the black car says one forty-five when we arrive at the church. The driver pulls to a side door where many people are standing, waiting, and watching—some I know like Aunt Lil, Miss Anna Lee, Miss Burler, three of Daddy's brothers and their wives, my teacher, Mrs. Faulkner, Reverend Isenhour and Mrs. Isenhour from the corner grocery store, and some people that I don't know, and have never seen before.

We all climb out of the car to go inside the church. I can smell dust and dampness in the old red brick building. It smells just as our house smells for a long time after a good long rain. We all line up and walk very slowly down the aisle past what seems like thousands of watchers mostly dressed in black and dark colors. As we walk closer up to where I can see my Granddaddy lying in the casket, I start to walk too slowly because my feet and legs feel so heavy like lead and like I can't pick them up.

Aunt Glenice takes my hand and halfway pulls me up the aisle the rest of the way. Grandma Allie starts to cry, and I start to feel guilty again. I feel like a killer returning to the scene of the crime. I turn my eyes without moving my head from left to right, and who do I see, Old Woman and Witch sitting on the row in the church watching me. Then, I turn my head; they are both gone. I suppose they had to be here at the funeral just for a minute, just like all the others, to see how Granddaddy looks, to see how I act when I see him—to see if I look guilty, if I might break down—just in case they need to do something—good or bad.

Flowers surround Granddaddy's casket—flowers on stands, round ones gigantic ones and little ones, flowers in pots sit on the floor on both sides. One large flower lies on top. Mama Allie stands at the casket looking at him and wiping her eyes every now and then with a lacy white handkerchief. Mama and Daddy take her away to sit on the front row right in front of where my grandfather lies. Aunt Florence sits on the other side of Daddy. Aunt Lil comes to sit beside Aunt Florence.

Now it's our turn to move closer—to see him. Now I see him. White shiny silk surrounds the inside of the casket where Granddaddy lies, like the kind Mama used when she made a dress one day for Mrs. Isenhour's daughter. Everybody says Mrs. Isenhour bought silk for her daughter's dress because she's rich. Daddy Claude looks like he's just lying there resting on that white silk in his gray suit, but his face looks dry and ashy, the way my legs look after my bath and before I grease them with Vaseline.

I keep very, very, very still while standing here at the casket, watching. Aunt Glenice is still holding my hand, not too tight but loosely now. She holds my hand and holds Uncle Horace's too. Uncle Horace is dressed in a black suit, and he's shined up from his wiry black hair down to his pointed toe shoes. He looks almost handsome. He stands here and shakes his head from side to side. He just keeps shaking his head. Aunt Odessa and her daughter, Niressa stands behind us with Ruth and Daniel, and they start to move near the casket. We start to move away.

We pass in front of my mama, Mama Allie, Daddy, Aunt Florence and Aunt Lil to sit on the front row too. So, Ruth, Daniel and Aunt Odessa and her daughter Niressa move past us to sit on the second row. I hope my sister will have the good sense to be quiet in here and not act the way she did while we were in the car coming over. You would think she would know better, or you would think that Mama and Daddy would tell her to stop. While we were in the car, they did not make her stop because they think she's smart and funny.

After they side step and slide into their row, they sit behind us. And I mean directly behind us—of all the luck! Aunt Glenice turns around in her seat, and takes Aunt Odessa's hand and holds it for a while, and I can see that Aunt Odessa's eyes are wet with tears too. I see that Mama is not crying. I wish she would hug Grandma Allie, because I see she's still crying. My Daddy has his arm around her again.

People are moving by the casket to see Daddy Claude and then by us. In passing, they shake our hands and kiss us saying, "I am so-so sorry." It starts to get very hot because Mama put too much starch in the cotton blouse I'm wearing, and it is scratching the back of my neck. And when these ladies that I don't even know— little old ladies Mama Allie's age, some wearing feathered hats pulled down close to their eyes; faces thick with powder. These ladies wearing gold rimmed glasses, and black square-heeled shoes, pucker their dry lips and lean down close to my face to plant a cold, wet kiss upon my cheek, all I can smell is talcum powder and Royal Crown hair grease on hair straightened with a hot comb. I feel like I might suffocate. And the old men smell just like cold salve—the kind Mama rubs on my chest to help me breathe and to get rid of a cold. I just don't know how long I can sit here smelling them; feeling like this and knowing in the back of my head that I am the reason everybody is here, and Granddaddy is lying there in that casket.

I feel like I'm going to burst open and all of the birds of guilt will fly out of my chest, flapping their wings into the air in the church, telling my secret. The quietness in the church is too much for me; I cannot help feeling that Old Woman and Witch just might come back to tell on me.

Before anything happens, the choir gets up to sing Hymn Number 41, and I feel saved for a while. As they sing, some women in white dresses and wearing white gloves called the ushers hand out a paper with Granddaddy's picture including his name on the front of it. They pass one of these papers with the picture to everybody in church, and everybody takes one including me. I don't look at the picture on the front because it's too painful. I open it right away, and inside it says: Going Home Service for Mr. Claude Allie. It says Mrs. Allie lay in bed in the late hours near her husband. Little did she know it would be for the last time. The paper tells Granddaddy's birth, Redwood City, California and the day he died, January 7th 1958—exactly seven days after I washed my socks. I am really starting to itch; I am really starting to get hot, and it's the middle of winter outside.

The choir has stopped singing, and the minister comes to the microphone to read what the paper calls the Scripture Reading, Old Testament, and while the minister is reading, I hear some old men behind us saying, "Yes Lord, thank you Jesus." Then a second minister stands, wearing a long black robe with red around the neck and a cross hangs on top of the red. Although I don't want to think of it because we're in church, I cannot help but be reminded of the red ribbon holding the seal on the bottle of Seagram's Seven. He reads the New Testament and says a prayer. I fold the program and use it for a fan. Then one choir member sings "Unspotted from the World." Her voice sounds tired and weak the same way she looks.

I open the paper again with Daddy Claude's picture on the front to see what is going to happen next and to see what happens last, so I can tell how long we have to be here. Deacon R. Bowman will sing Hymn No. 147; Reflections given by family and friends.

When then Pastor Lawrence begins the Eulogy, he says, he cannot preach Daddy Claude into heaven or hell. His life will speak for words; all he knows is life is over on this side, and Daddy Claude is surely gone to the other side. I suppose Daddy Claude has gone to be with Aunt Lillie's husband, Uncle Will and my little sister Sarah. The paper says after the Eulogy and Postlude, and the Recessional, then we leave for the Interment at the church cemetery. It looks like we won't get home until midnight. If this is the way of all funerals, I don't think I ever want to go to another one unless I just have to, even if it is my relative.

One, two, three, four, five, six, seven, and eight: Eight men in shiny black suits and shiny black shoes move to the casket. One of them picks up the flowers on the top and another one closes the lid, and the one who picked up the flowers puts them back on top again. They take my grandfather out of the church in the closed box, and I feel like I am locked in that box too—

like they have just taken a part of my heart with them inside that box because of the emptiness I feel inside my chest. Just when I think I can't stand it any longer, and my stomach starts to feel like butterflies are flapping their wings inside of it, and the birds of guilt are going to come out of my chest again, just in time the preacher asks everybody to stand and wait until the family leaves. We stand and start to leave the church by rows to go outside.

Outside the wind does not blow today; the branches do not move; outside is still and cold. Cold is on my face and in my eyes; my fingers start to feel numb. I put my hands in my coat pocket to make them feel better. People are coming up to hug and talk to the family. Some of them pat us on the back or kiss us again. They let us know whether they are going to the cemetery, and Mama tells them to come to the house later and get something to eat.

"We've got plenty of food over at the house now—all kinds of stuff. Make sure you come and help yourself." Mama says.

We climb into the black car again, and it pulls off to head for the cemetery. I press my face and hands against the window and watch the countryside as the big car glides along the streets, and for the short, quiet distance, I feel safe.

"People sure did turn out, didn't they?" Daddy says.

"Yes, they sure did," Mama answers him.

Ruth is quiet.

Everything is quiet as we ride along until I hear Daddy say, "I guess we'll go to Bent Hill on Sunday."

When the black limousine pulls up into Mama Allie's yard after the funeral, Miss Anna Lee is standing on the porch waiting. She watches us file out and began to go inside. Miss Burla from across the street greets us at the front porch too. She tells us, "We've come over just to sit with you for a while."

Come on in and have something to eat," Mama tells them.

From the kitchen stove, we pile food on plates, and take them to the dining room, the living room— wherever there is room to eat.

Talk of RW always began on this kind of occasion. Miss Anna Lee and Miss Burla don't waste any time putting their heads together at the dining room table. We hear them talk about the "situation." It does not seem to bother them any, that we are listening. Although they can never agree on the subject, their exchange of ideas keeps on.

Miss Anna Lee complains, "What is happening is far too dangerous for the Coloreds," as she taps cigarette ashes in an ashtray. "You know how the Klan threatened to kill the boys that kissed that white girl *and* their parents.

On the other hand, Miss Burla says, "Somebody needed to show 'the white man' we're not gonna' take his mess any more. We're tired of turning the other cheek. I think RW's fight for self-defense and respect is a good thing. Nobody else was gonna' save those little poor boys and their parents."

"But what if he causes one of your relatives to lose his life?" Miss Anna Lee asks, after coughing three times following a puff from her cigarette.

Miss Burla responds quickly, "The man put his *own* life on the line. Anyway, the Lord is in control of that. I don't think any of us are going before the Lord calls us."

"I guess you're trying to tell me that the boy who drowned in the swimming mud hole died because he was called?" Miss Anna Lee questions.

"I don't know about all of that, but I still think RW is a brave man for what he's doing around here, and all these here men should support him. Miss Burla adds.

It goes on like this until late—the conclusion is the same. To be continued until next time. The two of them became tired, realizing they both need to go home, leap up, throw their arms around each other, then Mama Allie, and the rest of the family; they drop their empty plates into the kitchen sink, and leave for home.

4

Daddy's suggestion after the funeral to go to Bent Hill on Sunday sure did go over as smooth as silk with Mama, I suppose because she didn't have the energy to put up a fuss, and I suppose she needed a change, to get away from Bright Town and the thought of Granddaddy's death. I am happy to think of something other than my trouble.

On Bent Hill my grandfather, Reverend D.A Wills, and my grandma Adessa on my father's side of the family, live on the other side of Highway 74 in Morris Town. Grandpa is a brother to Sylon Wills, who's married to Eloise Wills. Sylon and Eloise are RW, our cousin's grandparents. Today we're on our way to hear Grandpa preach his sermon at the United

Methodist Church of Bent Hill and then afterwards we head for what our family calls the "big house" for Sunday dinner.

At the big house, Grandpa Wills—we call him Papa, has over six acres of land surrounded by roads which triangle to major sections of Morris Town. In the summertime on Papa's land chickens run freely everywhere in the back yard, and hogs run around eating from the hog trough, and there is an old dog tied to a tree that always jumps up and down when he sees us. In the summertime apples, pears and peaches drop onto the ground from giant fruit trees that poke the clouds. Purple juicy ripe grapes hang on the thick vines curling around the wiry fence that surrounds the side path that leads to the plum trees loaded with sweet deep red plums.

I just *love* to go there when it's hot. But you have to be really, really careful and watch your step if you don't want to step on an overripe peach or rotten pear. Mama fusses all the way home if someone gets chicken or dog poop on the bottom of their shoes and smells up the car. I like to go barefooted in the summer time too, but it's no fun and a real strange feeling to have some of this rotten fruit squashed up between your toes or what's even worse is to get hit in the face with one by a sneaky cousin. It won't be as much fun today because it's January and it's cold outside.

Right after church, when we arrive at the big house, I always try to get a chair at the table before my cousins from Charleston, South Carolina do, because they don't like my sister and me and they call me "Gypsy Lady" in front of the whole family and everybody while we're there.

My cousins Mira and Judith like to sit across from my other cousin Barbara who lives on the Hill. They sit and exchange whispers and peeps at me. It makes me feel awfully uncomfortable.

When finally we're all seated, Grandpa Wills is at the head of the table with Grandma Adessa sitting queenly at the other end of the table nearest the kitchen. Then my daddy Jomis sits next to his father, and then there is my mama. I sit next to my mama and my sister Ruth sits next to me and our little brother Daniel sits next to Ruth. Then there is my Aunt Teddy and Uncle Andes and Barbara their daughter.

On the other side, next to Grandpa, are Uncle Hector and Aunt Amelia and their five children. Aunt Amelia holds their baby on her lap. My cousin Sylon III, Mira and Judith sit after Uncle Hector and his family. Grandma puts three tables together in the big dining room for the occasion. Aunt Joan and Aunt Lovie and their six children each usually sit in the kitchen at the table in there. This way they can help Grandma Adessa set out more food on the tables for the family.

Grandma Adessa's end is usually empty because she keeps disappearing to the kitchen. She's like a seesaw up and down, mostly busy the whole time, pouring more tea, bringing out bread, getting butter and her homemade jam for the table from Papa's curing room at the back of the house. She makes sure the pie crust is crispy and just right, and, "Do you want more chicken?" She brings more from the kitchen. "Do the children have enough? Now eat your greens child, so you will grow big and strong. Can I get you something?" She doesn't eat until everything is taken care of at the table and everyone is fed.

Seated at the table, Mama said, are three generations. Some of us have not seen each other for a long time. We're in the same family, but we're different in so many ways—by the way we talk, look and where we live. It sure is funny how this can happen; people from the same family that don't even look that way. My cousins from Charleston talk different from all of us. They have accents and talk funny, I suppose the way people talk from Charleston, like, will you broke the bread, child?

I get so tickled and look at my sister, Ruth, and she looks back at me in total amazement. And then my sister will say, "Yes, I'll '"break"' you some bread." We roll our eyes up to the ceiling and then to each other and stuff some more chicken and potato salad into our mouths. The next time I look up my spelling words, I plan to look up the people of Charleston in the encyclopedia, soon.

When we're visiting these relatives, it is the only time I really, really feel close to Ruth. At the big house, she and I become the allies of the stares against the enemy cousins. With those who live on Bent Hill side versus my cousins from Charleston, it's them and us.

My cousins from Charleston look a little like me. I think the real reason that they don't like us, especially me, is because we live on the Bright Town side of Morris Town. We talk real proper like my daddy taught us to because he "matriculated" to Shaw University and he knows a lot of, what Mama calls, ten dollar words that he taught my sister and me like: matriculate, harass and heathens.

I get really, really, mixed up over here on the Hill side because everybody is all mixed colors and all and look different from most of the other Negroes in Morris Town, and they look different from the people in my school, church and the Sunday school class too.

Papa Wills is white, at least that's what people around here says, any man with white skin, blue eyes and blond hair sure looks white to them. Grandma is Lumbee Indian; she has reddish-brown skin, silky black hair that hangs down her back to her waistline. Whenever she lets it hang loose, she can sit on it. My mama says she is mixed with Euro-American and the Blackfoot Indian of Canada because of her Native American father, and her grandmother, Mama Allie's mother, Maw, who was Euro and Native American, and who sat on the opposite side of Aunt Florence at the oil heater in Mama Allie's living room, Maw, who drank coffee, watched TV, and insisted until the day she died at age one-hundred and four, "I ain't got *no* 'nigger' blood in me."

My uncles and aunts on Daddy's side have light-light yellowish skin, green, gray, blue, brown or hazel eyes and some have red hair and some have real long black wavy hair like Grandma Adessa. One aunt looks Mexican with brown skin; green eyes and long wavy black hair flowing down her back. One aunt looks just like the movie star that played in "National Velvet." But I don't understand that either when she is supposed to be a Negro. She doesn't look like any Negro to me.

My cousins call me "Gypsy Lady", I guess because I'm light brown with long black hair to my shoulders. My daddy is lighter brown than I am, but he looks like a white man with his straight hair and all. He makes me sort of think of Clark Gable. So I don't know what to call myself. Sometimes I pretend to be White. Sometimes I pretend I'm all Indian. I *never* but *never ever* pretend to be a Negro though--not with all the problems in town about the Negroes,—and the negative things Whites say about *them* needing to go home, and how they make *them* go in the back door at the ice cream store up town and all.

When I let these words sink in my brain, 'Negroes go home', I think to myself, 'RW is trying to say, Negroes are home. My mama, Daddy, Ruth, Daniel and I were all born here.' I ask myself, 'what reason is there to make a law that requires a girl like me, wearing a pretty Sunday dress that Mama made for me, have to enter a back door just because I want an ice cream cone—AND, maybe a hamburger—with cheese and fries? This makes no sense to me at all. I want to go into the front door not only for something delicious to eat, but to show off my pretty dress to someone. No one *important* like the cute boy with dimples, my classmate, James, in Mrs. Faulkner's class, or Marshall the white boy who works in Reverend Isenhour's store is going to see my pretty dress that way, because I don't believe they would enter a back door either. Reverend Isenhour and Mr. Mangums, both white men, don't ask us to come in the back door to buy our groceries or *anything* at their stores.

At the big house, our appetites are fully satisfied with golden, crunchy fried chicken, collard-greens, syrupy candied yams, potato salad and Grandma Adessa's deep dish, homemade, green apple pie, green apples pulled right from the apple tree in Papa's front yard.

I see that Mama ate the fried chicken. I suppose she's thinking why turn it down when she didn't have the worry of wringing its neck or plucking the feathers.

After dinner the rooms in the house, especially the living and dining rooms are buzzing with my daddy, his brothers' and sisters' and their children's chatter. My brother Daniel and some of the other children have gone outside to run in the January air. Ruth has arranged for her friend, Christine, to pick her up and drop her off at the hospital for work. Before she leaves, she tells Mama, "I should be home before ten."

Papa Wills, a limp, tissue paper thin old man well into his seventies walks slowly using a cane to help him reach an old rocking chair, the back draped with a woolen afghan. It's located near the fireplace where he sits. An accident that injured his leg some years ago caused him to walk with a limp. The family follows him into the living room. As he sits rocking back and forth in the chair, he still speaks with authority about the Bible, his sermon, his six acres of land and his upholstery business—almost as if he is preaching another sermon. The flesh underneath his chin hangs low because of old age; it moves up and down with the emphasis of his words. His narrowing eyes are pretty, steel blue marbles. His soft, white, straight hair glistens like corn silk under the big ceiling light that hangs overhead.

He talks with pride. "You know my seven sons, some of you sitting here now, and I built this nine-room house with our bare hands right here on this land. And every **one** of you has your own plot right here to build on too." Papa narrows his blue eyes and turns his head around to have a look at his children. "You know Ella Rose and Andes, and Hulert, and Rosamuel have all built here." There are no interruptions from the family. *We are taught, when grown folks talk, we listen*. Children and adults sit and listen in the spacious living room, bounded with furniture and the smell of oak— sofas, chairs, tables of deep colors,—blacks, reds, blues and greens and the whitest of white curtains over the windows. The fireplace mantle is lined with faded out pictures of three generations of the family members.

Every Sunday gathering at the big house, when Papa's talk is finished, I know the turn the conversation will take as good as I know my own name. I can even say the words of the relatives myself—by heart. Sometimes, when I'm pretending to be white I do.

Uncle Andes, Uncle Hector, Uncle Rosamel, Uncle Hulert and my daddy, Jomis are sizing each other up to continue a Sunday debate. They sit in chairs making a church without a steeple with their fingers and twirling their thumbs around them in circles. Now and again one raises his eyebrows, tilts his head up slightly, just enough to steal a glimpse of the other, and just enough to give a peek of their green, blue, gray, hazel or brown eyes.

What I don't understand, but Daddy and the relatives know, is that this Sunday everyone was trying hard not to talk about the TV coverage of cousin, RW.

They are all going out of their way, making sure the family celebration does not become soiled by Uncle Andes' and Uncle Hector's hot tempered debate over the subject. However, the RW matter is locked into the hearts of the family, the town--the police, and the busload of Freedom Riders. The television reporter said that RW is the cause of all the commotion: When we studied the "D" and the "E" words, Mrs. Faulkner said: The concern is because a civil rights leader such as RW attempts to bring some dignity and equality to his people.

Finally, Uncle Andes with the bluest eyes of all stretches them wide. He stretches them wide since he knew he has the ownership of those blue eyes because he earned them just like Papa Wills. Like Papa, he and my daddy owned their upholstery businesses; that ownership earned Andes his picture in the yellow pages of the Morris Town telephone book. During "show and tell" civil rights study, I showed it to my classmates and Mrs. Faulkner. Uncle Andes stretches out his arms, and we know he is about to speak.

Then I remember the blue-eyed man down town who stretched his eyes wide when I mouthed off, like Mama, but I told some of the grown folks talk. I'd heard them say that the Waterworks charged the good "Coloreds" without reading the meter. Afterwards, I stood there with Mama as she paid the water bill. The blue-eyed man looked at me and said, "I wouldn't be going *round town spredin somum that wudduun, true* little gal." Mama had been telling me that my mouth was going to be my ruin. So I got right scared at what he said, but I didn't get scared at him for stretching his eyes, because I was use to seeing stretched blue eyes.

So Uncle Andes, the oldest, begins the conversation which is always the same; the subject they studied in school, and a subject RW's grandmother, Eloise Wills, and her brother-in-law, Papa use to read and discuss with them when they were young.

"The Germans during World War I." He says, "You know a German scientist created the pi R-square theory."

I move my lips like I'm saying the words with him. "Pi R-square theory."

He continues, "The Germans passed through several stages of development of which they were assimilators." He speaks with authority.

"Assimilation is just a process of adapting," Hulert suavely adds.

And I move my lips again. "Assimilation is just a process of adapting."

"Hector raises his head excitedly leaping at him, "And you interrupted Andes. Why do you interrupt a man in the middle of such an eloquent monologue?"

I say, "eloquent m-o-n-o-l-o-g-u-e" after he says it.

"For general principle." Hulert comments arrogantly.

"What is this general principal nonsense? There's only impulses my man, impulses." Hector is stretching his green eyes widely.

"Do you think WAR operates on impulse?" Andes, narrowing his blue eyes.

"Sure, it's publicity. For example, why does one German scientist try to wipe out one entire race of people from the face of the earth? No one could stop Hitler." Hector is excited and starts to stick out his chest and tuck in his chin taking in short deep breaths.

Andes shouts, "Hitler wasn't engaging in systematic knowledge. He was a mad radical."

I say "mad r-a-d-i-c-a-l."

Andes continues in his angry voice, "He tried to destroy the entire eastern human race for the way they treated him."

And I whisper, "Eastern human race for the way they treated him."

"Ah, the man wasn't smart enough to destroy a human race of people. He didn't even have a high school diploma," Hulert with the greenest eyes of all adds, calmly.

Hector, raises his hand in the air, waving it as if he is about to shoo a fly, "Mad rebel, whatever...."

His words trail off with the interruption of Aunt Loving's slow squeaky voice and long drawling southern accent. Up until now, none of the women folk had tried to compete in the continuous battle of the brothers.

"Hitler was just a plain fool. That's all he was – just a plain fool." She comes from the kitchen and walks over to the old red sofa near the fireplace. She wears a Sunday flower print dress and a brown sweater. The strong scent of Gin in addition to her kitchen smells of fried chicken and hint of onions surround her.

"Somebody take her back to the kitchen and give her another piece of pie." Andes complains as he would do anything to get rid of her.

Aunt Loving ignores him; she flops down on the sofa, crosses her legs at the ankle and sits a while. She continues. "Y'all talking 'bout the Germans. Don't you think you should be talking 'bout what's happening right round here?" She pauses as if she is waiting for an answer, but Daddy and the brother's heads are down; they don't respond.

"What do you think might happen to our cousin going with the Freedom Riders and trying to get service at the lunch counters?" Aunt Loving asks as she stretches her brown eyes. She seems to be trying to draw Uncle Andes in.

"You know it's public opinion and record,— known for years, that the Morris Town Country Club swimming pool is an important part of life in the county among white society. I hear that our cousin plans to take some Negroes to picket the pool next."

She adds. "It represents warm moist Carolina days of summer when children wish for a wet, inviting water hole. Unlike the unsafe one that the Negro children are accustomed to, the well-monitored, clean, blue water is well known to the white children, who're privileged to swim, give parties, play games, and engage in sports activities. Don't you'll think our Colored children deserve the same?"

Uncle Andes can't stand it another minute. He twists and turns in his chair until finally, "Ah Loving, we know what our children deserve 'round here!'"

Hulert chimes in again, "Even of more importance is the missed socialization for our young Negroes who hope in the *deepest* part of their hearts to be one to partake in the pleasure and privilege of dipping into that sweet wet summer bath and fun one day. Our kind-hearted cousin, RW just wants to provide this opportunity for the children—to *feel* the warm sun on their young backs, the wet, clean water, the experience of being watched over by a careful lifeguard sitting up on high, whose responsibility is to *serve* and *protect* them from danger as a divine being."

Rosamuel, widening his dazzling green eyes, and speaking for the first time, "BE REMINDED! It's a commonly known truth that Negro lives are repeatedly lost to those swimming holes, muddy creeks and rock quarries, especially in the heart of a teary-eyed mother, who has received the horrible news of a drowned child she hugged just hours before. I *know* our memories are not obliterated of poor Monford's mother, right over there on Tobye Street, in Bright Town, when they brought his DEAD body home, after he drowned in that dangerous, unsupervised swimming-hole. You *know* that **ripped** our hearts apart."

I listen, then repeat his words, "obliterated." My heart aches to learn about a poor boy drowning who lived on Tobye Street in our neighborhood only because he was a Negro and couldn't swim in the white swimming pool. *That's* why I don't *ever* want to call *myself* a Negro. I tell myself.

"It's a shame that integration to the white community is a threat by Negroes; mixing in the water of a pool supported by our tax dollars is forbidden and protected by "White Only" signs and Separatism by race law," he adds.

Lovie jumps in again, "The White folks say he's goin' round here stirring up stuff? Y'all watch yourselves; don't none of you mess around and git yourself killed fooling wid him." She looks over at Jomis, knowing his intention to become a part of RW's riffle men. "These white folks don't want to give up nothing. Old man Woods down at that corner store acted *real* different the other day when I went in to buy a bag of flour. He just kept looking at me and all—like I'd done something. Then he finally asked me what I thought of *them* Freedom Riders being here in Morris Town. I didn't know what to say. I finally told him, I don't know." Aunt Loving looks like she is fixing her mouth to say something else, but before she has a chance Uncle Hulert stops her with his words.

"That's enough talk about that, Loving!" Uncle Hulert says, and searches around the room with his eyes, witnesses the young relatives' keen attention; he is ready to end any more talk about the subject of R W.

There is silence. All of the brother's heads are down and twirling thumbs again; they're in deep thought. And for a short while, there are no more flickers of blue, green, gray or brown eyes.

Grandma Adessa finally breaks her silence. In a kind, sweet sing-along manner, she says, "There's plenty more pie in the kitchen. Y'all help yourselves." Then turning to my mama, "Martha, don't you want another piece of pie?" My mama says she believe she will and moves to the kitchen.

The silence overtakes the room. The only noises are the grunting sounds of the hogs that drift into the window from the pen in the back yard, the smaller children playing and the fire crackling in the fireplace.

With Mama gone, seeing this as his chance to speak without her contradiction, my daddy, Jomis, tries to be the hero of the occasion; we hear him speak, and I move my lips to his words too. "When I matriculated at Shaw University, I intended to conduct a detailed study concerning the Hitler mentality and if the British refusal of involvement was simply a matter of right verses wrong."

Hector, who had been standing and warming himself by the fireplace, was now less emotional. "Neither Hitler's psyche nor the British indifference was a matter of ethics; it was a matter of dominance, information, connections and weapons. If anything, it's just the opposite—a lack of morality. Hitler didn't have one ounce of ethics."

I repeat, "A lack of morality--morality."

"He would have slaughtered Jesus had he been around during Biblical times. And for the British, why during the years of British imperialism, social control was the chief concern for the British monarchy. They denied the basic ordinary political and civil rights of existence to anyone that was not a part of the kingdom. British values and Nazi beliefs were quite similar in fact."

I say, "British; monarchy; kingdom; Nazi."

Mama returns to the living room with a piece of pie on a saucer twirling her fork in the air in the other hand. And I just know she is about to mouth off just by the way she is looking at my daddy. So I push out my lips and bat my eyelashes just like her when she is about to speak. She says, "Jomis, did I hear you say you were going to study something about Hitler?" She sits down and starts to chew on a piece of apple pie.

Before my daddy has a chance to answer, he is saved by Uncle Andes who hotly criticizes and who my mama is not about to mess with. "Do I detect that another *female* has attempted to enter this conversation?" Before anyone has a chance to answer, he adds, "I think I'll take a walk out onto the front porch. It's impossible for a *man* to get a word in edgewise around here with the womenfolk butting in. Don't you all have enough recipes and babies to talk about?" He gets up and walks out of the front door and closes it behind him.

Mama is determined to try to get in some licks before he leaves. But she's too late. She yells after him, "It's not that a man can't get a word in. You men just want to control us."

Everyone is quiet again, and I'm thinking the trouble with Mama is that she never knows when to hold her tongue. It seems like I know more about that than she does. No wonder she's always talking about how my tongue will be my ruin some day. I guess she knows all about that. I suppose that's one thing she sees of herself in me. So she warns me every chance she gets. I wish she would take her own advice because she can't get anywhere at all with Daddy running off at the mouth like that. I know Papa Wills wishes she would be quiet like most of the other women. He just looks at my daddy like he's saying can't you keep her quiet? And Daddy just looks out done, like he can't do anything with his wife. They don't care when Aunt Loving as they say "butts in" because she's usually had too much Gin to drink or "spirits" as Daddy calls it.

With the battle of my uncles over for now, my interest turns to the porch with Uncle Andes so I put on my coat and go outside too. The two of us just stand on the porch looking across the land at the other houses, Uncle Andes house and upholstery shop across the street. I cannot not help but think of the fun Barbara and I might have if the other cousins weren't here dividing us.

After a while, Uncle Andes lights his tobacco pipe that he held in his hand puffs on it and blows the smoke into the air. I form my mouth in a circle, blow in the air against the wind and see the smoke too.

Just as we are about to go inside, Daniel and our cousins come running up to the porch completely out of breath. "A police car is coming in the driveway." The boys run up onto the porch and Uncle Andes puts his hand up to his eyes like it's helping him see.

Sure enough, a police car stops and a policeman gets out and walks up to the porch where we all stand. He takes his hat off and holds it in his hand. He speaks to Uncle Andes. "There were some boys with some guns in this area. We're looking for them. Have you seen any boys with guns around here?"

Uncle Andes holding his pipe in his hand says, "No sir, we haven't seen anyone with guns around here, sir."

The police officer looks all around then says, "Well if you see anybody looking suspicious, you be sure to call us and let us know, will you?"

My uncle answers, "Yes sir we'll be sure to do that."

The police officer turns to leave then he turns around again suddenly and points to my cousin standing on the porch with my brother Daniel. He points his finger toward my cousins Jason and asks, "What would you do if a big bear ran right up here after you?"

Jason says hastily, "We'd shoot him."

Without hesitation, the police officer asks. "Well now what would you shoot him with?"

Jason answers, "We got some guns in the house." He points to the house. The police officer walks up the steps, onto the porch, and to the door and opens it. "Show me the guns boys," he says.

My cousin leads the police officer into the house and we all follow them to the fireplace mantle where Jason points.

The officer walks to the mantle and picks up the two cap pistols my cousin received for Christmas lying there. He acts like he's examining them carefully. "Don't hurt nobody with these guns, you hear?" He says before putting them back onto the mantle with all of the family watching, including Papa Wills who has now gotten up from his chair.

The officer turns to Papa and says, "There was some trouble in the area with some boys and guns that we're looking for. Y'all be careful now. Good day." He walks out the front door and closes it behind him.

Papa Wills grabs my cousin, Jason, by the arm and starts to give him a good hard shake. "Don't be so 'pleg-teggit' fast!"

I start to move my lips, "Pleg-teggit, pleg-teggit."

Andes sits down in his chair, steaming. "That police officer knows he wasn't looking for no 'dat blame' boys in this area with any guns. He wanted to see what *this family* is doing!"

The debate has given the brothers delight. The policeman's appearance provokes arguments all over again. Everyone—including Mama and the aunts, start to speak at the same time. They go to the kitchen, where they stand talking. I hear one say, "The police knew *we* are the relatives of RW." Another says, "I suppose he had to give a report down town about the family's activities." Still, another states, "He saw that we are respectable men and women, with our parents and children at our side."

The brothers pull out the pint bottles that they, at first, hid from Papa, and some take sips of *brown* and others take sips of *white*, as they eat more chicken, more pie, and finally tiptoe and teeter back to warm in front of the grate, at the fireplace. Uncle Hector starts quoting the German he knows: "Mein Vater fragte mich nach den Apfel." Then he says it again, "Mein Vater fragte mich nach den Apfel."

I say, "Mein Vater fragte mich nach den Apfel."

Uncle Rosamuel begins quoting scripture from the Bible as Andes listens. "A man's life: *Three Score and Ten*; Jesus at 13; Mark I."

I say, "Jesus at 13. *Three Score and Ten*, a man's life."

Uncle Hulert starts to incorporate humor into his explanation of world affairs: "How big is the Washington Redskins practice field? Don't let your head get the size of that field when I'm teaching you something you don't know"-- right in the middle of telling Uncle Silon to listen to how to install a water heater. "You remember when I gave you that cap pistol for Christmas when you were a little boy, don't you? I told you, don't kill nobody with it, didn't I?"

I could feel the love; we are joyous until late hours when we wave good-byes and return, sleepy and tired, to our own homes.

5

It's the beginning of February, three weeks after our trip to Bent Hill. I still feel exhausted from everything that's happened. I complete my class work, put my head down, thinking about Valentine's Day coming, but although my head is on my desk when she calls my name, Mrs. Faulkner, my teacher chooses me to take a note down the hall to Mrs. Clegg, my sister's teacher. I'm so tired, but I don't plan to pass up a chance to speak French to Mrs. Clegg. Daddy taught Ruth some big French words when she was five years old. He wouldn't teach me any of them because he said

I was too little. I listened real *good,* and so I learned them anyway. I can say really, really, proper like, "Bon Jour Madam, Como tele voo." I need Daddy to teach me how to say Happy Valentine's Day in French.

My sister Ruth hates to see me coming when Mrs. Faulkner sends me into her class with a note. She **was** only three grades ahead of me in school; she is suppose to be only two because she's two years older than I am. But she's smart so Mama started her to school early. She is so smart that the principal, Mr. Charles let her skip a grade too; so now she is four grades ahead of me. This is the reason she and her friends think they know everything "grown" because they're in the ninth grade, and they think I'm a little kid—they say a real brat, which is what I heard my sister's best friend Christine tell Ruth one day. They didn't know I was listening.

Mama must have heard my wish since she dresses me in skirts and blouses even on cold days instead of that brown snowsuit that suddenly disappeared. Today I'm dressed in my woolen green skirt trimmed in red around the edge. My hair is all braided in long braids that hang down my back with a ribbon tied on the end of the plat that's on the top of my head. So with the note in my hand I walk into Mrs. Clegg's ninth grade class and walk up to her desk and say my French, "Bon Jour Madam, como tele voo." I look over my shoulder to where my sister sits behind Christine, and Christine's friend Jewel, sits beside her and two other girls older than Ruth sits behind them.

There they are the four of them staring at me like they can look right through to my heart and tell that I have a problem and I'm scared about something. Since they're looking at me so hard, I think of something to say to get them concentrating on something else. I make sure they are still looking at me when I ever so slowly hand Mrs. Clegg the note. Now, I ask Mrs. Clegg in a kind of low voice but just loud enough for the class to hear me, "May I speak to ARCHIBALD?" And I turn and point to my sister, Ruth. Everyone in the classroom gives Ruth a long stare and bursts out laughing. Some cover their mouths to try to keep from laughing. Mrs. Clegg says, "Now class, let's get back to work." She just nods her head giving me permission. I walk over and lean over close to Ruth and whisper, "AR-CHI-BALD, how are you?" Before she can even catch her breath to say anything, I turn quickly and make my way back to her teacher's desk to get the note that she is sending back to Mrs. Faulkner.

Archibald is such an ugly, awful name! But this is the only way I know of getting back at Ruth for what her best friend Christine does to me at school. Whenever Mrs. Faulkner has to leave the room and needs a student to keep the class, Mrs. Clegg always sends my sister's friend, Christine, because her mama and daddy are both school teachers too. Everybody tries to be her friend at school *except* me. So she doesn't like me at all and welcomes any opportunity to say that I was talking while the teacher was out, so she can hit me with Mrs. Faulkner's leather strap that she uses to keep the class in line.

When Christine hits me, she intends for it to hurt, and it surely does FOR REAL. But I'm not about to let her know it. So I pretend that it doesn't hurt. And whenever I act like it doesn't hurt, she hits me a second time—this time much harder—and this time taking the smile right off of my face. But this is as far as I am determined to let her get. I refuse to let her see water come into my eyes, which is what she wants so badly to see.

She says, "You're a stubborn little brat aren't you?" I just stare at her, which she hates because she knows I can stare her down, too. I can stare her down because I stare Uncle Hector down when he stretches his green eyes to try to make me blink. So I know how to stare even blue eyes down. Sometimes I practice staring into Uncle Andes blue eyes until we both just get tired and quit when Daddy takes us to Bent Hill, or when I spend time in Uncle Andes' upholstery shop with my cousin, Barbara, his daughter. I can stare without blinking, so I *always* stare Christine's brown eyes down.

She really doesn't pick on the other students the way she always picks on me. And I'm sure that it is NOT because of anything my sister has told her that would make her not want to be nice to me. Ruth likes to pretend big and uncaring about me around her, and she likes her friends, but I *truly believe* she likes me more; and for some reason she just doesn't want me to know it. I suppose it's all about being all grown up and the sappy kid stuff like making over your little sister. But I know deep in my heart that she would have a fit if I really told her about what her friend Christine has done to me. Christine knows that Ruth had better not ever find out that she hit her little sweet sister 'cause she would surely light into her like lightening striking, and Christine would have to run for the hills. If I had a little sister, I know that I would never allow someone to hurt her. If anything, when it came to outsiders, I would take up for her all of the time like I honestly know Ruth would take up for me.

Well, it turns out just as I knew it would. Ruth might take up for me when it comes to outsiders, but when it comes to her and Mama, she just can't keep her mouth shut. Just as soon as I get home, Mama is waiting in an uproar for me and lights into me with all fours. Ruth told on me. Mama knows all about how I showed out in her classroom today, and how I called her Archibald", *which, now that I think of it, happens to be a good and lovely name for her*. Anyway, she told how the whole class laughed at her.

I try to explain to Mama that I didn't set out to hurt my sister, and I say under my breath, "Archibald." I wanted to explain to Mama about this thing with Granddaddy and how it has me doing stuff that even I can't understand. "I didn't intend to call Ruth out of her name." I tell Mama, "I was just playing and teasing her."

None of this works. Mama's mind is made up. "Emilee, I'm going to whip your behind. So you march right outside and get a switch, bring it back and then take off that skirt."

I'm beginning to feel pretty sorry for myself. Mama has an iron arm when it comes to whippings. It takes a long time for her to get tired. Before I leave to get a switch, I want Mama to know that she never whips Ruth like she does me. So I yell out to Mama, "Ruth's friend Christine hit me with Mrs. Faulkner's strap, and I hadn't done anything to get hit either." I start blabbing about how all of us in Mrs. Faulkner's class were talking, but Christine only hits me, and that she hits me more than once, and that she hits me hard—two times, and it hurts really, really bad.

Mama insists that I must have been doing something like showing off again no doubt, in class like she says I always do. "Otherwise, Christine would not have hit you at all for no reason." She asks, "Now why would she just pick you to hit, Emilee? Why?"

I yell in my defense, "Because they don't like me, Mama." Mama demands that I shut up now. I keep talking—giving her word for word. "I didn't tell you everything on Ruth. I didn't tell you that I saw her on the back porch kissing Jude and smoking a cigarette the other day after school. They didn't know I was standing in the kitchen watching and listening. I heard Jude say he could put an Aspirin in the cigarette to make them feel high." I didn't really, really mean to tell this, but it is too late because *these words fly out of my mouth like a bird that suddenly finds a cage door open.*

These words make Mama get up at this point and start coming in my direction. I don't know what to do, to run, to hide or stay here. Something tells me running would be a bad idea when she catches up with me. I know I can't hide because when she finds me she would kill me for sure. My life is flashing before my eyes, and like an idiot I stand here. When Mama stands in front of me, she slaps me across my face with the iron hand. For an instant, I feel a sharp stinging pain on the left side of my face, and I see stars. I not only see stars, the breath is knocked out of me and I lose my balance and stumble backward landing on the sofa and quietly sit here for a while trying to get my breath back. When I realize that I won't be hit again and how badly my face hurts, I really start to cry.

Mama turns leaving me here on the sofa and walks away. She seems to feel satisfied, and she forgets about telling me to get a switch.

The tears that flow into the pores of my face finally dissolve away, as only minutes later I lay curled on the sofa. Before falling into a deep kind of dream, I decide I will run away from home. I'll leave on Valentine Day so Mama and Ruth will always remember and never forget how they teamed up against me—hurt me.

In my dream, I walk in between Old Woman and Witch and then sit with my bare feet in the chilly water miles away at Richardson Creek. I listen to the calming sounds of the wilderness around me as the Old Woman and Witch ponder the question of what I should do.

"Mrs. Isenhour at the store will know what to do. You should talk to her. Rich ladies are good, always smiling and know which path to take," Old Woman retorts.

"Mama might be mad if she finds out that I told a white lady about my troubles," I say.

"How's she going to find out, unless you tell? Then she will surely scold you." Witch grunts.

Secretly, all I can think of is how deeply I envy the closeness that *Martha* has with Ruth. (In my dream, I can't stand to call, Martha, Mama right now). I know I am willing to do anything to please her, to help an improved understanding. I'm willing to cook and to clean and run errands to the store, I can help Daddy in the upholstery shop, pull tacks out of his work shoes so he could be happy for *Martha*; I can scratch her head when it itches--anything. But, the possibility is unlikely, especially now that I have caused *Martha's* father's death. And this unfortunate problem is getting in the way of everywhere I go, everything I do and think. There is no way of getting around it; as a cloud looms in the sky, it looms over my head; my happiness is all gone. The only thing left is to disappear—unless—unless, Mrs. Isenhour does have a way to save me, to give me something to be happy about once again.

But if, indeed, I do have to run away, have to leave Morris Town, maybe; just maybe, it could be with the bus load of Freedom Riders. I, too, can go around fighting for freedom. I can be the youngest person in history to travel the world fighting for freedom. After all, there were both Negro and White fighters. I can do something great for the poor little Negro children-- great like Martin Luther King and RW, fighting for the right to swim in the summertime in a safe pool. Then, *Martha* would be sad that I'm no longer at home when she hears about the news on television and neighbors inquire about my whereabouts. Then *she* would have to tell them, "My daughter is in Africa fighting for Africans; she's in London fighting for people there, she's in India fighting for the Indians, she's in Mexico fighting for Mexicans."

I smile in my dream, no one except Mrs. Isenhour could believe I would do something so important and out of the ordinary for all the countries I read about in the history book. In my dream, I float above these countries, the states, the cities and towns including Morris Town.

"Emilee, Emilee!"

I jump; sit straight up on the sofa feeling like I might still be dreaming, when I feel *Martha* shaking me. It is warm and perspiration dots the pores of my forehead. I'm fully awake now, and it is *her*, (She doesn't know it, but I still cannot bring myself to refer to her as my mama, right now).

Martha commands, "Get up, Emilee, supper is on the stove."

Valentine Day comes and goes without much happiness. At school Mrs. Faulkner handed out construction paper and coloring pencils to make Valentine cards for our parents. Then she gave us all kinds of candy bars and sandwich cookies to eat during class. Vettie made a valentine card for her mother; I made one for my teacher. I'm still upset with Mama, I mean *Martha*.

6

My thoughts of talking with Mrs. Isenhour about my troubles with Mama, Ruth and Christine and running away with the Freedom Riders are left behind in my dream when we're all awakened by Mama Allie early one morning. I can call Martha, *Mama*, again, because I suddenly realize I'm not the only one who has trouble—Mama Allie has worries too.

"Lord, here comes Miss Allie down the path." Daddy is standing and looking out of the window. We all jump out of bed fly to the window and pull the curtain to the side. Mama Allie looks like Red, her old hen, with his wings spread half flying half running, when he's chasing somebody down the path. Her housecoat is wide open and she still wears her mixed salt and pepper hair twisted around her pink sponge hair rollers underneath her black hair net. She holds her arms in the air and I'm reminded of an airplane about to take off for a flight.

Even before she makes it to the porch, we can hear her almost out of breath. "Get up, Get up." In a low hoarse voice still filled with sleep, making sure not to talk so loud that she would wake up the neighbors, especially Miss Anna Lee, who lives directly across the street, and is sure to come to see what the commotion is all about.

Mama and Daddy both run to the door. Daniel and I almost knock Mama down running too, and we stand right behind Mama. Daddy opens the door; Mama pulls Mama Allie in. Daddy tells us, "Get out of the way. Don't y'all have to get ready for school?"

"Lord have mercy, Martha." Mama Allie flops down on the sofa trying to catch her breath; she's crying and talking at the same time. "Lord Jesus, your crazy brother." She starts crying again before she gets out what she is trying to say, as she wipes her eyes with the edge of her housecoat.

Daddy sits on the sofa beside her, "Take it easy. What's the matter? What happened Miss Allie?"

She points her finger at my mama and shakes it. "Your crazy brother! I told him to get rid of that motorcycle." She keeps talking. "I told Glenice she needin be ridin round here wid dat darn fool, encouraging him and all. Y'all know we already got plenty of trouble to deal with round here."

And before she has a chance to say anymore, Mama interrupts, "What happened to him. Calm down and tell us, Mama. Were they in an accident or something?"

"No, no. I *were* in a deep sleep when that sheriff called my house a while ago, and Glenice's gone lookin for him."

Mama, standing near the heater, rushes to Grand mama's side, "Well what happened? Why did the sheriff call?"

"Lord, Lord, LORD! That crazy fool's gone and got drunk. He got a hold to some of that 'ole bad liquor again at one of them juke joints. He knows he c'an't handle that stuff. I wish the folks round here would stop making that 'ole crazy juice. And dat's another thang too. Dat boy won't listen to Jesus 'hisself'. The sheriff says that now he's gone and rode dat motorcycle and took that rifle while he was drunk, and they claims he's done shot out some of them blame signal lights down there where he works at the Seaboard Railroad Station. And now 'dey lookin' for him. And when dey do find him, Lord *help* him! 'Dey gone lock him up, and 'dey gone throw away the key!" Mama Allie sits there with anger curled on her lips and disgust on her face as tears flow like blood from her eyes.

Mama is the first one to speak. She had been sitting with her head in her hand as she listened to

Mama Allie. "Why that crazy fool! He has lost his mind for sure. Well, where is he now?"

"He calls 'hisself' hidin'. And Martha, you know they ain't playin wid his be-hind dis time. You know that's that same sheriff that came to the house before Claude died during the raids. You know he's still mad 'cause he couldn't find nothing on us. So he's got it in for Horace. He wants to put somebody away." Mama Allie's tears start flowing again. "Claude warned Horace time and time again bout his actin' a fool wid that 'ole gun and drinkin that white lightning. He ought to know; the sheriff **told** him the last time he got into a scrape with the law...that the next time dey's gone send him way from here--up yonder to 'dat prison. He knows dat."

We all listen and my heart is with Mama Allie's heart. I can't stand to see my grandma cry like she's doing now. I feel like I can't do anything to help her, and I think about my plan to talk to Mrs. Isenhour about running away. But there is no way I can do that now—not with Mama Allie and Uncle Horace needing me and all. No! I can't leave them now. I decide I have to stay right here and fight for my family instead of fighting for people all over the world.

"Well where do you suppose he is? He ought to know where ever he is they gone find him." Mama says to Grandma as she turns and tells us, "Get in there and get ready for school, both of you. Go on Emilee, Daniel." So we leave Mama Allie's side to move to the kitchen.

"I don't know what the big fuss is about anyway. Y'all know how Uncle Horace gets sometimes." Ruth, who is dressed for school, says, and she shakes her head and talks like one of the grown folks in matters like these. I can see and hear her from the kitchen. "Mama, what do you think they'll do to him?"

And while they ponder over her question, before anyone has a chance to answer, I hear the front door open and close when Ruth leaves for school.

Daniel and I do what Mama tells us to do. Daniel finds his socks and shoes, and starts to put them on. I go to the back room to finish getting ready for school. But while I'm dressing, I stay quiet so I can listen to what I'm not supposed to hear. I dress as slowly as I can and listen as long and hard as I can.

I hear Mama ask her mother, "Mama, what would make him do something so crazy? He ought to know he can't go messin with his job like that. Especially with all the mess that's going on around here with those Whites and the Coloreds scared they're going to lose the jobs and all. I saw him pass the house a few days ago, and he seemed all right then."

According to Mama Allie, "It don't take much to set dat fool off when he's been 'drankin." But she says, "The real reason he was madder than a hornet was that he found some papers in one of Daddy Claude's old trunks." When I have to get my shoes from under the bed, I miss a bit of the conversation, but I hear Mama Allie tell Mama—"I had to tell your brother the truth."

On the verge of tears again, and I see her wiping her eyes with the end of her housecoat she continues, "I wanted to keep from having to say those words, but I suppose it was time. Horace had to be told. He needed to know that Claude's not his real daddy. And all this time everybody thought he knew, like you and your sisters Florence and Odessa."

Mama Allie's voice went up and down, at first with whole words and then chopped up ones broken by tears. She was worried about Uncle Horace's wife and children—how they might have to take their hard earned money to get him a lawyer from up there in Charlotte, and how, no matter what they do that the sheriff would send him off anyway.

"You know 'bout when they got to fightin' over yonder at 'Big Sixes' place, (that Morris Town Speakeasy), and somebody called the law," she said. "Dey was drinking and fightin' in dat 'ole jute joint over there across the tracks too, where he wants to hang around at night till wee hours in the morning. It's a miracle that he still has that good job at the station."

When I'm dressed for school, I go to the kitchen to get some grits and butter that Daddy fixed for breakfast and a biscuit left over from last night's supper. I stand at the door with my bowl. I take a bite of biscuit, and eat a spoon of grits and listen. I hear Mama Allie say, "Horace was like a wild man when I told him that his daddy was an old man who died while all of you were little. He just plain blew up when he found out Claude didn't leave him anything in his will and that he didn't leave him any of his personal belongings."

"I had to tell him that Claude has a son in Redwood City, California, that he left his personal affects to—his gold watch, his two gold rings, and his gold false teeth. An insurance policy worth five thousand dollars was left in my name that no one else knew he had except me." I hear Mama Allie say, "I told him, Claude's son worked on the Transcontinental Rail Lines that ran from coast to coast and belonged to the Brotherhood Locomotive Engineers."

I repeat in a whisper: "Transcontinental Rail Lines and Brotherhood Locomotive." In my mind, it's hard to get it in my brain that all this time, I thought Daddy Claude was my uncle's father. No wonder he was always mad at Daddy Claude, but he just didn't know why he was so mad. I sure wouldn't want to suddenly learn something like that about my daddy. No wonder Uncle Horace had gotten all drunken up on crazy juice.

Then Mama Allie says, "Horace just couldn't understand how a son wouldn't come to his own father's funeral, that he must not be much of a son." She said Uncle Horace was mad that Daddy Claude would leave something to such a son. The last thing he said was that, "he would have come to his own father's funeral even if he had to crawl to it."

7

As I sit here on Grandma's step drawing pictures in the dirt with my stick, I'm trying to figure some things out: How I lost my socks; I'm worried about Uncle Horace being lost, but I'm thinking of Mama and Daddy too.

"I'm going to Kansas City. Kansas City here I come. They got some crazy little women there, and I'm gonna get me one"—I'm thinking of Daddy singing this song.

I'm not sure about this, but I don't believe Daddy is too happy about Mama's old high school boyfriend just showing up at our front door for a visit. I heard Daddy call him competition one day. Competition—I've got to remember to look this word up in the dictionary. I'm drawing it in the dirt on the ground with my stick so I won't forget it—competition. I wonder if Daddy's competition ever held Mama's hand. I just can't see Mama ever holding anybody's hand but Daddy's. I know Daddy sure didn't like him though.

It's easy for me to tell when Daddy doesn't like something or someone too, because of the frown on his face-- three wide lines across his forehead almost as wide as the lines I'm drawing in the dirt with my stick. He won't get nervous, and he won't say any curse words like *shit*, *hell* or *damn* either like I heard Uncle Horace say whenever he went to Hog Pen Hill. Uncle Horace says he learned his cussing in the Army. I suppose Daddy knows how to put up a "good cussing," too, because he's been in the Army during World War II just like my uncle. If they wanted to, I bet both of them can definitely put up a good swearing after a bottle of Seagram's Seven. I'm writing *shit*, *hell* and *damn* in the dirt. Whenever Uncle Horace finds his way back home, he sure is going to be thankful he won't have to go to the hog pen now that Daddy Claude is dead and gone and I'm certain Mama Allie won't be raising any hogs.

When something bothers Daddy, he just won't talk much. He is real quiet, so how he felt about Joseph Pines was as plain as the lines were on his forehead and these lines I'm drawing in the dirt. Mama called him J-

O-E. I'm drawing *Joe* and making him *"ugly"* with a big nose, raggedy teeth, pop eyes, and elephant ears!

Mama said she could have married either Joseph Pines or my daddy. She said Joe was a very religious man and had a habit of stopping, pulling off his hat, getting down on his knees and praying, no matter where he was or who was watching at the time.

I don't believe it for one minute, but Mama said she wished 'the Lord' she had known about the kind of man my daddy was. She said she didn't know that he had "funny ways" and that he was hard to get along with and that she can't get him to fix the chairs in the house. He fixes everybody's chairs in the whole town except ours. I know this fact myself. Daddy has an old torn up sofa still sitting against the wall of Ruth and my room since before Christmas—before Thanksgiving, that he hasn't fixed. Mama says our chairs are the "raggediest" ones in town.

Too bad, Mama said she can't get Daddy to pick up his clothes or put his plate in the sink after he eats supper. She said he got his old habits from his old daddy, Papa Wills. This makes me confused, since I see my daddy cooking my mama's breakfast—flipping flapjacks on the stove on Sunday morning and then taking them in to her, before she gets out of bed. And I hear them laughing together all of the time in their room behind the closed door. When I grow up and if get a husband, I hope he won't act the way Mama claims Daddy does.

But the only time I know that Daddy really won't listen to Mama is when she tries to teach him about the pressure cooker. BOOM! Is what we all hear. Then, after that, we hear Daddy say, "Dog gone it. I thought I

had that '"thang"' set just right. Martha, didn't you tell me to put it on five pounds of pressure? I thought I set it just like you told me to." Then he tells Daniel, "Bring me that chair so I can clean the beans off the ceiling. This wouldn't happen if you chaps and your mama wasn't harassing me all of the time. You're just a bunch of scalawags. You won't let a man think around here. Hotahmighty!"

On the day that Joseph Pines came, I saw him pull up in front of our house in his shiny blue Buick. I knew it was a Buick because Daddy has one too, but it's an old one. So I ran down the path to home. I made sure I beat him getting in the house so I could see what might happen. I rushed past Mama; sat right down on the sofa.

Mama told him, "Come on in and sit down."
He was still standing, "I was up the street visiting my Aunt Jane, and thought I'd stop by to see you all." He looked at Daddy as he talked.

Mama asked him, "You want to take off your coat?"

He took off his long, blue overcoat and handed it to Mama. She hung it by the door.

Joseph started to rub his yellow hands together real fast, like he was rubbing two sticks to start a fire; I guess he was warming them. He sat down on the sofa. "I heard about your father passing. I'm sorry."

Mama returned, "Thank you."

Joseph continued to talk, "You know Aunt Jane has been sick with high blood pressure, and she came home from the hospital today." He looked around the room and said. "You're looking well, Mart." He smiled.

The lines across Daddy's forehead got deeper when he heard Joseph call my mama "Mart", short for Martha. My daddy never calls Mama that. He sometimes calls her Mae, for Martha Mae, but never Mart—not a name that she had shared with Joseph Pines when they were younger and still in school.

Joseph Pines was a tall, yellow and handsome, successful business insurance man who had gone to live up North according to the folks around here in Morris Town that talk to Mama Allie. And they say at first he just kept waiting around for my mama, and he didn't marry until after my mama got married to my daddy. And after Joseph Pines did marry, he named his son the same name that my brother has. All I can think of is that Joseph Pines could have ended up being Ruth, mine and Daniel's daddy. Ruth might grow up having his big hands and his big feet to match. Daniel might take after his height. But me, I don't know what I might have except his color 'cause that's just what I got from my daddy.

Daddy asked Joseph, "How's your family—your wife and son?"

"They're both doing just fine as can be, Jomis."

I suppose Daddy was talking about the *red bone* (a very light skinned female) from DC the people say Joseph Pines met while he was in school at Howard University that Uncle Horace talks about. Grandma said she thinks the real reason Mama married my daddy is because he's a preacher's son and, had light skin like Joseph Pines but my daddy has that *good* hair. Miss Brewster, the music teacher at school told me one day, "If I had your last name I would write it on the chalkboard so *beautifully*."

Joseph Pines coming to town to pay Mama a visit always stirs up a whole lot of talk among the men folks. Afterward— when he's gone, the men: Uncle Horace before he shot out the railroad lights and disappeared, his brother-in-law James, and my daddy were in the back yard under the Pecan shade tree. Uncle Horace use to say all the time, "You know they say they got some fine looking women up there at Howard.

Then James, Uncle Horace's brother-in-law says, "Jomis it's just like Shaw. You know what the women looked like at Bennett right up the road from where you were. They wouldn't even let them in the school 'less they had that *l-o-n-g* hair, was light-skinned and good looking."

Mama just couldn't stand to see Daddy, Uncle Horace and James with their heads together under a tree because she said she knew they were talking about the women from Daddy's college, with Uncle Horace grinning from ear to ear so hard that his teeth were piano keys. The news about Mama's old boyfriend coming must have spread to the other side of town to Bent Hill because Uncle Hector pulled up in his old grey Chevrolet truck that afternoon with the engine knocking, rattling and smoking, with Andes sitting on the other side and Hulert and Rosamuel in the back. They all came to swap stories about the news of both Joseph Pines and R.W and share in the talk. And every once in a while they stopped dead in the middle of a sentence when they heard a noise like my mama or Aunt Glenice coming around the corner of the house.

They talked from early afternoon until early evening, until the shadow of the Pecan tree was a skeleton, extended across the rooftop of our house. They talked of what is in the hearts and minds of the townspeople's latest information. The news of RW's promise: To fight against the white people because the Coloreds didn't have any protection from the white man around here. They talked of RW's promise to the newspaper people that the Coloreds would defend themselves, and how the NAACP up yonder in New York believed in self-defense too.

Although Daddy had gotten with the men folk to talk about the women, I could tell he still was not too happy about Joseph Pines coming here. When I got up at 7:30 a.m. that weekend he was already up and dressed and standing in the kitchen with a coffee cup in his hand on a Saturday morning when he usually sleeps way pass nine. I knew he was a little mad when Mama came into the kitchen and he turned his back to her and stared out of the window and started singing.

"I'm going to Kansas City, Kansas City here I come. They got some crazy little women there, and I'm gonna get me one."

When Daddy finished singing, he sat his coffee cup down on the kitchen cabinet, Mama said, "Like he was making a statement." He gave Mama a hard look and went out the back door, got into his Buick.

Mama called after him, "Jomis, you going up the highway to Sanford's?"

Daddy backed out of the yard, pulled off without saying a word. Sometimes on Saturday, he goes to his weekday job up old Charlotte Highway, and then he comes home around two or three o'clock in the afternoon to work in the old shop in the back yard sometimes way past midnight. I knew he would be back soon because he had four chairs and a sofa to finish for that nice white man, Mr. Michael, who works at the downtown courthouse. He gave me a blue and gold writing pen that said Board of Education when he came here to pick up one of the chairs Daddy covered. Even Mama said he was a nice man, and she doesn't just take to anybody just 'cause they're white she says.

Mama looked outdone when Daddy pulled off without talking to her. She seemed to be crying inside without tears. She finally said, "I guess he'll be back here before too long."

I walked outside to be with Frock where he was tied up. He looked outdone too. He just turned around and hung his head down low before he lay down on the

ground beside his doghouse. I guess he, too, figured Daddy would be back soon.

****

I hear our dog Frock howling and Mama crying. Daddy came to the house from work at the Old Charlotte Road, but he passed the house and kept on going, sneaking over to Bent Hill, I guess, to be with his brothers, Andes, Hulert, Rosamuel and Hector on a Saturday night. I suppose Mama is crying because Daddy has been gone since the morning, and he didn't even stop and come in after work. And I suppose Frock is barking because he wants to go to Bent Hill with Daddy. I believe Daddy thinks this is the best way to punish Mama for Joseph Pines showing up.

Mama cried and Frock howled half the night. And for the rest of the night, she spent it packing her bags. I heard her packing and slinging things every which a way. She made so much noise, packing, slamming drawers and talking to herself that I don't see how she expected anybody to sleep. I don't know which one was worst, her packing and crying or Frocks howling.

Daddy finally comes home at five o'clock Sunday morning, and I get up. She tells Daddy after he comes in, "I'm leaving you, Jomis. And there's nothing you can do to stop me." Mama has two bags packed and sitting by the door.

When they hear Daddy come in, Ruth and Daniel get up out of bed, too. They both dress and head for

the kitchen. I start to go to the kitchen too, as I see Daddy sitting there in a chair near the door looking at Mama. He looks real worried. His eyes are wide. He and Mama sit staring at each other like they're communicating with their eyes, and as I pass Mama reaches and grabs me and pulls me closely to her chest and tells Daddy, "When I go, this is the only child I'm taking with me."

Daddy gets up from where he's sitting and grabs Mama and me and holds us real tightly. Mama cries some more, and as Daddy holds us, I smell cigarette smoke on Daddy's breath; I feel my mama loosening her hold on me and leaning into Daddy like a cloud moving behind the sun, and I know the trouble between the two is close to being over.

****

The first words out of Mama's mouth as she meets us at the door when we come home from school today is that our dog Frock broke loose from the old rusty chain he was tied with. And Mama says that he has probably turned over every trashcan in the neighborhood that had anything worth eating in it. She says she just hopes that he hasn't bitten anyone. It is already four o'clock and nobody has called Mama Allie's house to tell her to tell Mama anything, and nobody has come by to report any damages to any property or anybody bitten yet. So she says we need to hurry up and find him. I don't dare go looking for him in my good clothes. Mama wants us to find him right away, though.

It's March, the back room is cold and it isn't easy to find a change of clothes, but I find my blue Khaki pants and put them on as quickly as I can ready myself to go with Ruth and Daniel to find Frock.

After I change clothes, I go to the kitchen to get a biscuit and Mama is still talking. She just keeps talking as I make a glass of sugar water to drink with my bread.

"I don't have any money to pay for anybody's doctor bill if he bites somebody."

The only time Frock breaks his chain is when a stranger passing by might say something to get him mad or if he gets in heat. The last time he was in heat, we didn't find him until the next morning. We didn't find him, though; he just came back home and was sitting on the front porch when Daddy left early that morning for work. When he breaks loose, he roams the neighborhood, turns over the trashcans and drags smelly stuff home, like a dead bird. Sometimes Frock goes as far as Richardson Creek.

The man who lives up the street, Mr. Manning, said Frock is a dangerous animal and very likely to bite some child someday if we aren't careful with him. To tell the truth, I wouldn't mind if Frock did take a little plug out of him. Then he might stop trying to meddle in everybody's business. Miss Anna Lee says nobody can stand him. He's an old junk man with all kinds of stuff and gadgets at his house. One day Daniel had to stop him from taking his bicycle wheel. When he stopped in the yard to pick it up he first examined it, sniffed it, rubbed it and then started to walk off with it. Daniel told Mr. Manning, 'You just put my wheel right back where you found it.' He took Mr. Manning by surprise.

Anyway, it seems like the only reason Mama really keeps Frock around is so he can keep an eye on Daddy. As soon as Frock hears the motor of Daddy's old Buick, it seems that he has two special kinds of signals. He starts to bark to let Mama knows that Daddy is coming home, and he howls to warn Mama when Daddy is trying to get away from the two of them. I guess Frock calls himself running away, because he's unhappy about Daddy not taking him on Saturday night over to Bent Hill too.

Frock usually runs away down to the Seaboard railroad tracks, Hog Pen Hill or down to the garbage dump. After checking Hog Pen Hill and the railroad tracks, we find traces of him at the garbage dump. There is a group of other dogs grinding their noses into the stinky, smelly garbage, and it seems that Frock might have been suspicious that we are on to him, so he cuts out early to throw us off his trail. Too bad we don't have his dog sense and aren't able to sniff his trail like he can ours.

On the other side of the dump there is an old, rusted out truck, and sure enough there is Frock sniffing around in the truck bed. We can tell he is happy to see us. He jumps at first like he is about to run, and then his ears go up into a point. His bobbed tail pendulates from one side to the other in fast motion, then he twirls it a couple of times.

Ruth commands "Come on, Frock! Come on, boy!"

And he climbs down and follows my sister as we all walk down the road to home. He gallops at first like a horse, and then runs. He acts like he's on a secret mission, running around, looking for clues to investigate, poking his nose into every hole and behind every crack he finds—sniffs it and decides to either explore it further or move on.

Mama found Frock one day and just brought him home. She takes everything in that doesn't have a home—a cat that finally had five kittens (two were born Siamese-joined at the side. They died). She gave the other three away and the mother soon got old and died too. One day she brought home a large cooter she found crawling down the street. Daniel wanted to keep it for a pet. But Daddy got a big thrill out of cutting it out of the shell, and then he cut the heart out and head off, then boiled it all day and tried to fool us in to thinking it tasted, he said "just like chicken." I couldn't stand to think about it. It made my flesh crawl just like the two Siamese cats. Ruth told me she had to cut up a frog in her Biology class. That too made me gag.

Mama said she doesn't know whether Frock is what you call full-blooded pedigree or just a mutt. I don't see what difference it makes because they all seem the same to me. It seems like they all do the same things—eat, bark sometimes all night, sleep and sometimes run away.

Sometimes while walking home, Frock has his nose low to the ground as if to say, *now, why did you have to come and find me. I was perfectly happy with what I was doing and here you come.* He seems sad to be going home to, as Daddy would say, his restricted area and his confining ropes.

We round the corner of Winchester, and the old house where I was born, and Frock breaks free and races up to the back steps barking like crazy. We call him to come back, but he acts like he is trying to tell us something. But no one has lived in that old house for a long time. Frock scratches at the wood shed, and we go to have a peek. Sure enough, Frock has located a familiar scent. There, lying on a blanket asleep and stinking with some gnats flying around his nose is Uncle Horace.

We call to him, and Frock keeps barking and starts to run all around him and lick his face. We try to get him up with our yelling, but it seems he's just too weak and sleepy. Uncle Horace keeps telling us, "Let me alone. Let me alone." He brings his legs up and forms a ball with his hands between them.

We finally get Frock to stop barking and come away from under the house. We leave Ruth and Frock with Uncle Horace. Daniel and I make our way home as fast as our legs will carry us to let Mama know that we've found Frock and that Frock has found Uncle Horace.

As soon as Uncle Horace crawls from under the wood shed and stood on his weak legs, he, Ruth and Frock make their way to Mama Allie's. A sheriff's police car appears in the yard out of nowhere with lights flashing that light up the whole neighborhood.

"We've been looking for you Horace; everybody move back out of the way!" A big red man yells out of the car window as he and the other sheriff spring from the car.

Uncle Horace stumbles back and forth still trying to get his legs to work. By now Miss Burla, Miss Anna Lee, Mama and Mama Allie have gathered around him; Ruth, Daniel and I stand watching from the porch with Aunt Florence. Frock barks nonstop in a roar; Ruth holds on to him.

"Turn around now boy, and don't give us no trouble you hear; we have to take you in for shooting out *dhem* lights down yonder at the railroad station."
We watch him reach behind himself, pull out the handcuffs, turn Uncle Horace around and put the handcuffs on his wrists. He doesn't put up any struggle, and he is walked over; put in the backseat of the sheriff's car behind what looks like a cage.

We witness what we did not wish to see, I am terrified, even spellbound with fascination, but ashamed all at once.

Miss Ana Lee and Miss Burla both tell us, "I'm so sorry; but it's getting late," and they leave for home.

I suppose Mama Allie is thinking Uncle Horace's crime finally catches up with him just as she predicted. She stands here crying an old woman's chilling cry that rings in my ears. I suppose she is thinking about her words, *"Dhey gone lock him up and throw away the key."* I did not want to watch. The strangeness I feel inside my stomach and chest is different from before not like the flapjacks being tossed—but pity—pity for Uncle Horace who now sits handcuffed in the backseat of the sheriff's car with his head held so low we can't hardly see him; it makes him seem so small—invisible. I suppose Jim Crow has sent the sheriff after him; *maybe to kill him.* In my mind I can't help but call on the Lord—secretly I hope for Witch and some of her magical powers to whirl him away so he won't be locked up. I can't bear to think that he might be killed for what he has done—shooting out some lights.

Now Mama Allie's worry is the safety of her *only* son—"the son", she says, 'who went off in the United States Army to fight in the government's war over seas and came back bringing family honor--a son who *never* met his real father.'

"He's had run-ins with the law from time to time, but never spent any "real time" in jail. He's not a bad son, he just *do* what many young men *do* these days."

I know she saw him as her progeny and would not spare time or money in keeping him out of the Morris Town jail.

She tells Mama, with a tremor in her voice, "I don't want to leave him in that jail; dem Klans might take him during the night and hang him just for sport. What *is* we gonna do? I hope it's not too late for us to help him tonight."

Mama agrees, "No telling what might happen to him tonight. Jomis is going to have to tell Glenice that he's been picked up by the sheriff."

As they stand pondering over what will become of Horace, the sheriff is heard radioing downtown. "I'm bringing in that boy Horace Allie." We hear the radio dispatch say, "We'll be standing by, ten-four!"

The sheriff's car pulls off; I watch the white men pull off. We all stand on the porch, Mama, her mother and Aunt Florence anticipating going inside, Ruth has already gone and taken Frock to tie him up again; Daniel and I about to walk down the path. Before we move there is a movement in the yard—and we notice this movement and there is a sound, but it's dark, too dark to see by the moonlight and one street light; so we walk over to see what animal might be there—I believe perhaps its Miss Mae Lee's cat, the one that disappeared and has been gone for months has finally returned, or Witch might be trying to tell us something to help my uncle.

Our eyes fall upon the ground and to our amazement; we see something shining by the moonlight. There curled in a ball and hiding beside the large, black wash pot that sits on the ground on one side of Mama Allie's yard, the one that Mama uses to build a fire under to boil our clothes to get them clean. We stand here in a daze; there is a figure, but it's not the cat—it's not Witch, nor Old Woman. We see silver glittering handcuffs dangling from one arm. No one can speak at first. Mama peers around and over her shoulders. We discover Uncle Horace lying there.

Mama whispers "Help him up! Help get him up!"

We all reach for Uncle Horace's shivering body to help him stand up on his legs. While Mama, Aunt Florence and Mama Allie hold on to him. In another whisper, as they walk him to the porch as quickly as possible, "Don't tell anybody about this, Emilee, you and Daniel go on home!"

We both "hightail it" down the path like we're being chased by wolves. When I reach the porch and look back up the path, Mama, Mama Allie, Aunt Florence and Uncle Horace are not there.

At home, the first thing out of Daniel's mouth before he hardly makes it inside the door, huffing and out of breath, "Ruth, you won't believe who we found again...?"

Ruth is all ears.

8

    I come home for lunch today tired from tossing in bed half the night thinking about Uncle Horace, and the smell of Pinto beans hits me at the door. I suppose it was the quickest thing Mama could cook today after she and Mama Allie were up so late last night.

    When I grow up there is one thing I do know for sure. If I ever have children, I'll *never* make them eat a pinto bean, especially if they have rocks in them. Mama has a habit of just jumping up all at once and dumping the whole bag of beans into the pot, and not take the time or won't take time to pick the rocks out of them, like she does when she's in a hurry. I hope Mama at least put the beans on the stove early enough to get good and done before it's time to eat them.

I suppose Mama has too many chores to do and too much to worry about around here than to waste time finding a recipe for cooking beans, or reading the directions on the package before she tries to cook them. I read the bag they come in, and it says: This is a natural food of the earth; we suggest you carefully rinse with fresh water as you would any fresh vegetable, and sort any pebbles or foreign matter before cooking. On the stove are neck bones and greens, corn bread too, and in the middle of the table is a big glass pitcher of ice tea.

I wish I didn't have to come home every day for lunch. I wish I could eat in the cafeteria at lunchtime. The food smells some kind of good. There were cream potatoes with cheese on top, and green beans, some kind of hamburger meat in the gravy that Daddy says was Salisbury steak, and peach cobbler for desert, on the one day I ate there. A lot of my schoolmates eat in the cafeteria every day. Their parents must have a lot of money. Ruth doesn't come home for lunch much now that she has gotten an afternoon job working in the cafeteria at the hospital. She mostly eats with her friends at school.

Daddy comes home for lunch every day. By the time he gets home though, we're leaving to go back to school and by then the beans are well done. I think my daddy comes home sometimes so he can spend time with Mama. Today Mama looks like one of those ladies in Life magazine. She has arranged her hair, and she's all polished wearing lip stick and high-heel shoes. On these days she fixes the extra stuff to eat with the beans.

I believe Mama is trying to make up for all the worry Uncle Horace caused Daddy, when she and Grandma took Uncle Horace downtown last night.

Lately, I've heard my parents arguing at night about what RW is doing, and how dangerous it is for Daddy to be involved. But last night I heard them talking late into the night about what happened to Uncle Horace—how Mama Allie had to take him downtown to the police station in Mr. Albert's taxicab before that sheriff discovered him gone and before he returned to the house. She had to call a lawyer at his home to come to bailed him out of jail, and now he will have to go to court, not only for what the sheriff claims, shooting out the lights, but his disappearing from the sheriff's car too. I think Witch and Old Woman had something to do with that, after I called on them.

Today, Mama is wearing Chanel # 5, the perfume Daddy gave her for Christmas; she keeps it in a box of her favorite things that sits on her dresser: broaches, pearls hairpins, ribbons, and perfume. I'm reminded of Mama when we lived at the top of the stairs in the two-story house on Winchester—her sitting in her room in front of the old oak dresser, combing her hair and painting her lips. She was so slim, dark and polished with even white teeth, and she looked even more sparkling in her red, silk dress, that she wore out to the dance with Daddy at the Winchester community center.

Mama had many, many boxes of favorite things, as many as ten. And when she wasn't looking, and I had a chance to, I sprayed myself with her perfume and wore her pearls and broaches. When I sniffed myself it made me happy to smell her perfume on me.

When Daddy comes home and finds her all made up, he won't be in a hurry to sit down at the table to eat. He won't wash his hands in the kitchen sink either like he usually does. He'll smile at Mama in a kind of special way and go to the bathroom to wash up right before we leave to return to school. Mama is smoking a cigarette; she holds her lips in a pucker, then she blows the smoke out lightly away from the table like she's on a Lucky Strike commercial.

Sometimes though, if Daddy comes home for lunch early enough, before we eat together, he has each one of us repeat Bible verses around the table. I know a lot of Bible Verses because of Mrs. Allgood's Sunday school class at Friendship Baptist Church, and because my teacher Mrs. Faulkner requires the class to read and memorize the Bible verses and the Ten Commandments. Every Wednesday Mrs. Faulkner has us stand in front of the class and say the verses we're assigned exactly as it's written: including all the thee and thou and thus. She gives us a grade for it too. Today, at the table before lunch if Daddy comes early, I'm going to say the first part of the Commandment that tells us how we are supposed to honor our parents. I suppose this is the reason I'm not scared to talk in front of the class. Daddy has us talk in front of him all the time.

Last week I had to say this verse, *"Make a joyful noise before the Lord..."* in front of the class at school; Mrs. Faulkner brings copies of all kinds of books and magazines to class. I read in Seventeen Magazine that women with hairs on their legs shave them off with this real pretty pink shaving cream. I counted fifteen hairs on one leg and fourteen on the other. The night before school, I shaved my legs with Daddy's shaver and Ivory soap. As soon as I walked up to the front of the room, this boy called T-H said, "Look at her legs." The whole class, including Vettie started to laugh and make fun of me; I felt real silly.

I ran back to my seat. Mrs. Faulkner tried to encourage me go back; she even threatened to give me a
zero if I didn't go up and finish what she calls "the presentation". But nothing would make me budge. I don't think I like shaved legs anymore. Let the white girls do that. I sure don't want to go through what the boys put me through again--made fun of by the whole class. It was surprising to me that the boys even noticed my legs; after all, I only shaved a few hairs off. I suddenly discovered that boys must notice everything about girls and what we do.

Frock is barking to let Mama know that Daddy is pulling into the yard for lunch. There's one thing for sure. Daddy won't ever have to worry about anybody being glad to see him as long as he has that dog. Frock is jumping up and down and carrying on like somebody put a steak bone in front of him.

Daniel comes in the house too. He heads straight for the kitchen stove and starts to lift the lids on the pots and pans.

Mama tells him, "Go to the sink and wash your hands." The lids are hot and Daniel burns his fingers and stands there shaking them over the stove. It seems like Daniel hates to wash his hands worse than anything else, because he gives Mama an "I want to eat" look. But he finally does what he is told.

"You wouldn't have burned your fingers if you'd done what I told you to do in the first place, Boy." She says.

While Daniel washes his hands, I put the plates and forks on the table.

Daddy comes in and blesses the table "Lord Jesus thank you for this food and for these our bounty we pray, Amen." He tells Daniel and me to go ahead and eat. Afterwards he and Mama go to the living room to sit together on the sofa. We can hear them laughing and talking while we eat. Daddy's laughter with Mama, I believe, tells me he has gotten over Joseph Pines' visit, but now he has to help Mama with Uncle Horace?

****

It's windy today, almost too windy to draw in the dirt with my stick. But I'm sitting here after school on the porch step drawing anyway. I look up and the clouds have moved in right over the house, I guess bringing an April shower. Just as I look up, taking my eyes off of my drawing –I always end up drawing a picture of a house with a chimney and smoke curling out of it—suddenly I hear a popping—what sounds like firecrackers, five or six of them going off all at once. I can't tell what direction they're coming from.

I jump up and twirl around and the clouds send down what Mama calls sheets of rain, in very large drops with balls of ice too. I run down the path as fast as my legs will carry me to get out of the rain. I hear what sounds like firecrackers again, only this time I believe the sounds are gunshots; and this time I feel something hit me in the top of my head. I'm weak. I stumble to the porch crying, "Mama! Help me, Mama!"

Mama must have heard that little whisper because in an instant the door is open, and she comes running to the porch, "Emilee, what's the matter?" she says; She holds the door opens, grabs my hand and pulls me into the house.

As I stumble onto the sofa. "HELP ME MAMA! HELP ME! I'VE BEEN S-S-SHOT." I say. And it's the last thing I remember for a while. When I wake up later still lying on the sofa, Mama and Ruth are standing over me. With both hands, I feel my head where I know there should be blood, and it's wet from getting shot.

Mama says, "It's only wet from rain and a ball of hail hit you in the top of your head while you were running home."

Then I discover wetness elsewhere. With my hands, I discover that there is blood, but it's not on my head. The blood is on both of my legs. Mama says I *"started."*

Ruth says I'm now a little woman; she takes my hand, leads me to the bathroom and gives me one of her thick white pads and shows me what to do with it. Then she tells me, "Walk normal and stop walking so wide legged. You look like John Wayne."

I do feel different, though. I feel strange. When I pass the mirror on Mama's dresser, I take a good look at myself. I don't look like *no* woman. All I see is my same face. The storm is over, but I don't feel much like going back outside to play. Besides, I'm wearing this thick pad Ruth gave me, so I decide to lie on the sofa to watch TV.

The storm is over in the sky, but the news on the TV says some Freedom Riders and the Negroes have been arrested for going where the Chief of Police say they should not go, to the lunch counters, and the restaurants thinking they can get some service.

<u>9</u>

I was feeling sad for myself because I mostly have pinto beans for lunch, and Vettie mostly has chicken, rice and biscuits with gravy, cake with Jell-O and Kool-Aid for lunch, mostly left over from supper the night before. But I just can't believe what she found when she went home for lunch on Monday. Poor Vettie.

I know she must somehow feel like I felt when Daddy Claude died except he died in his bed because of me. Daddy Claude didn't shoot himself on the back porch with his own gun, and I didn't come home to eat lunch and find him there.

We could just about set our clock by Vettie's father, Mr. Belling, who cut his grass at nine o'clock every Saturday Morning. I don't know how it will seem now not seeing him wearing his suspenders that held up his pants and pushing his lawn mower over the yard, pausing now and then to wipe sweat from his face with his handkerchief. I don't know if anybody else in Morris Town wears suspenders; everybody I know like Daddy, Uncle Horace and Granddaddy before he died wore belts to hold up their pants.

Vettie's oldest sister, Yolanda who has two babies, who lives in the house with them, too, used to pay me a dollar to scratch the dandruff off her head. Sometimes on Saturdays, she let me curl her hair for two dollars. I don't think I can do that now, I mean go over there knowing what I know about the back porch and all. They're still planning to stay—I mean live in that same house and sleep there too. But of course, when my little baby sister died, we didn't move, but the thing about it is that my little sister, Sarah, just died in her sleep. That's different from a grown person causing himself to die. If I hear noises, I might jump right out of my skin—not to mention if I see a shadow or something. I might think Mr. Belling might be coming back for something.

People around here do believe in ghost, but I do not. But, I surely am getting goose bumps on the back of my neck now just by thinking about them. I don't plan to make up any test either to see if they really do exist and if I really do believe or not. I was doing my spelling. We're up to the Ps but I dropped back to the Gs to look up the word "ghost" in the encyclopedia, and it said according to tradition, it is a spirit of a dead person that visits the living. It also said most ghosts are malevolent. That is, they try to do harm and are usually thought to be the spirit of a person who was murdered or harmed by relatives or friends.

I get it now. That's why that woman came back looking for her head in the story Uncle Horace told us. She came back because she was murdered—her head chopped right off by her lover. The book also said most people do not believe in ghosts, but some do and that reports of seeing or hearing ghosts have been common throughout history.

I sure hope that Mr. Belling wasn't mistreated by any of his relatives—like his wife or one of his other children. I'm sure he won't be coming back because of anything Vettie did. She is one of the sweetest girls I know. Most of the time when I see her, she's smiling a wide grin. Her father must have been awfully unhappy. I wonder why.

If I close my eyes and in my mind, I can see Mr. Belling's whole body standing in their yard just as I can sometimes still see my Grandfather sitting on the front porch. I blink and these images are gone just like the real people who left. They are here one day and gone the next. Life sure can do some funny things, especially with people you know and people you love.

I don't know whether Vettie and Mr. Belling were as close to each other as Daddy Claude and I were. Sometimes I truly believe my granddaddy could see around corners, predict the weather by the ache in his foot and tell who was knocking at the front door without having to peep out through the curtains, as the rest of us had to do.

Once Granddaddy said, a stranger was coming to the house because of the way his hand was itching, and it sure did come true, just as he said it would. An old white man, dressed in a brown suit, selling some kind of expensive Hover vacuum cleaners in big boxes knocked on the door and tried to get Granddaddy to buy one. Mama Allie said he was a door-to-door salesman. He told Granddaddy and Mama Allie that he would show them how it worked if they let him come in and clean the floor. However, Daddy Claude told him no. Sometime Granddaddy said it would rain even when the sun blazed, then a dark cloud covered the sky and it would pour down rain. I wonder if Granddaddy knew in advance about anything that might happen to poor old Mr. Belling or if he knew anything about how the town would be in trouble. I wonder if he knew about the Freedom Riders or anything at all through his mind, his heart or his stomach, or if he could tell by the way his eye twitched or how his hand itched. All I know is that it sure is different around here without him and poor old Mr. Belling.

I suppose I can say that Vettie was my best friend. We mostly played together after school some days and on Saturday. At first we were real close until she got a glimpse of Marshall, the grocery store boy, who works at Reverend Isenhouer's store, smiling at me. It really made Vettie mad to see him ride his bicycle to my house and spend time after he delivered a package up the path to Mama Allie's house. Mama Allie says she's too old to walk to the store anymore to get her own package of meat. She usually calls Mr. Albert's taxicab to take her. But when she cannot get a cab, sometimes he already has passengers in the car when he shows up, then she calls up to Mr. Isenhour's store, and Marshall has to deliver the order.

He sure is cute to be a white boy. He's the only white boy I've ever noticed and who has ever noticed me. His hair is blond like Grandpa Wills' was. Now Grandpa Wills' hair is all grey. Marshall's eyes are blue just like Grandpa Wills' and Uncle Andes's eyes. So, looking and talking to him wasn't hard and didn't make me nervous either, not even when he smiled at me. I had on my short shorts and a pink shirt. April is a good month for wearing shorts. We didn't talk about much because he didn't have to ask my name, since he already knew it. He knew me because Mama sends me up the road to Rev. Isenhour's store sometimes, but mostly she sends me to Mangum's. Marshall and I mostly just stood looking each other over, but he did ask me what grade I was in and how old I am. I told him, "I'm in Mrs. Faulkner's fifth grade class and I turn twelve next month." I didn't want him to think I'm a baby or anything. So I told him, "I read in our history book that in some countries like India and Africa, girls can get married at twelve, but *I* wouldn't want to."

He said he's fifteen going on sixteen in December. And before too long he finally said, "I'll be getting on back to the store now." And he rode his bike off and up the road. After Marshall talked to me, and her father died, Vettie didn't come out to talk to me anymore. She might have thought I was "walking on the edge" as the old people say when you do something dangerous. She might have thought it was dangerous for me to talk to a white boy because of the trouble between the Whites and the Negroes.

Anyway, Vettie began talking to Ronda Budd, another classmate. It sort of hurt me that we weren't friends anymore, and I haven't found a new one, and it doesn't matter because I still have my sister. Now it's just me left to get along with Ruth. Vettie doesn't have a sister in school. She only has one brother.

Easter is coming; today the news reporter on the television said it's like the whole town has gone wild. Most of the picketing is taking place right on the steps of the downtown courthouse. A white woman and a black man attended a church downtown. Gunfire rang out; marchers were hit and Negroes were being spit on. Negroes were carrying guns too! Freedom Riders marched in front of hostile crowds of Whites and a young Negro boy was beaten and hospitalized. Picketers were battered and bruised by angry mobs of whites carrying the rebel flag. The news says after RW carried some Negroes to picket the all white swimming pool nothing has been the same. The white people say they can't swim in the same water that Coloreds have been in. They will have to drain the pool if used by Negroes.

Mama says to stay indoors and that Daniel and I can't go away from the house after five.

We're not sure how my brother managed to get past all of us and out of the house, but around six-thirty, before any of us realizes he's gone, Daniel comes running into the house out of breath. He doesn't stop until he reaches the kitchen where Mama sits at the table. His shoulders moves up and down as he sucks air into his nostrils and tells Mama, "A man on the corner—- in a big car stopped--- pulled out a bottle and held it out the window in one hand with a gun in the other. He told me, drink this pint of liquor, boy--- or I'll blow your head off."

Mama grabs Daniel's shoulders. "What!" She inspects him, and seeing that he is not hurt, she shakes him. "Boy, what did you leave this house for? We told you not to go out didn't we? Now get over there and sit down!" She slaps him on the back of the head when he turns around.

Daniel yells, "Oh!" He grabs the back of his head with both hands as he sits on the floor near the sofa.

Around seven o'clock a special report says: The police chief is *leading* the KKK through the streets. He later claims according to the locals, he is doing this so he can help keep order.

Soon Daddy comes home from work and he doesn't waste any time. He turns out the lights in the house again and tells us, "Stay away from the windows and lie down on the floor because the Klan intends another ride through Bright Town. They might shoot at the house or throw rocks and bottles through the windows."

The five of us—Mama, Daddy, Ruth, Daniel and I huddle together on the floor, and all we hear are loud yelling voices outside, and the thunder of motors from automobiles. Lights flash against the room from lined up cars moving down our street. "There must be as many as before. What looks like hundreds of them,"

Daddy says, "heading again toward Dr. Phelps house to bomb it."

I was asleep on the floor when I awaken and discover the Klan ride is over. I can see that all the lights are turned on again; Mama tells me to go to bed. But when I don't see Daddy, I ask his whereabouts. Mama tells me, "Your daddy has gone up the path to see if Mama Allie and Aunt Florence are safe."

Daniel is already in bed, and Ruth is on her knees looking out of the window. Before I traipse off to bed, I ask Mama, "Will we go to school tomorrow?" She tells me that school should be open and we should be going. I am glad to climb into bed and began drifting off to sleep.

The front door opening awakens me and I turn over in bed so I can listen. Before I drift off to sleep again, I hear Daddy come in from seeing after Mama Allie and Aunt Florence. Uncle Horace is with him. It's the first time he's been here since Mama Allie bailed him out of jail.

I hear him tell Mama, "The folks up and down the street are saying that RW and his defense squad were waiting in ditches and sandbag trenches with firearms when the KKK motorcade arrived and started firing their guns at Dr. Phelps' house. Only this time they were met with RW's Armed Defense Squad firing their guns into the air."

Uncle Horace finishes the story, "When the Klan unexpectedly heard gunfire, and motorcade cars came close to crashing into each other. They scrambled with the steering wheels trying to turn them around and sped their cars off in another direction to get out of the line of fire. Those white cowards were glad to get out of there alive, and they haven't returned."

He says, "Everybody up the path is in bed and probably asleep by now. I believe it might be safe to go back down the street to my wife, Glenice, and the children."

****

We're studying about civil rights in Mrs. Faulkner's class: *Brown v. Board of Education,* that racial segregation in public schools is unconstitutional. If it's unconstitutional, then I wonder why are we separated from going to the nice white school? I didn't ask this question because Mrs. Faulkner would have given us more homework and everyone in class would have blamed me.

I wondered why the KKK is riding through our neighborhoods. Why are they trying to hurt us? That makes me feel so bad. But, Easter is coming soon, and maybe I'll feel better then. Mama is making me a pretty dress.

10

I come home today, and find my green socks washed, rolled together and lying on the foot of my bed with my skirt and sweater. They are staring at me like some puppy that's run away and finally returned home. Mama must have found them, although she doesn't know anything about them being lost in the first place. Now that I think about it, it's almost as if they have come back from the dead to give my secret away—to haunt me.

I had given up on looking for them and was even glad they had disappeared. And now I have to admit my problem all over again to myself. Here they are to prove that I've done something terrible, and I need to get rid of the evidence as soon as I have a chance. I'll wait until tomorrow, when Daniel has gone to play with someone up the street and I'll bury my socks right near the longest root of the Pecan tree in the back yard.

****

Poor Daddy Claude's been buried for three months now, and my socks have only been buried for one hour. I'm sitting here on Mama Allie's front porch step holding a stick in my hand; drawing pictures on the ground in the dirt just like nothing has happened--trying to think of something good and not think of bitterness—Grandma Adessa's green apple pie sure is a good thing to take my mind off the bad stuff.

Thinking of Granddaddy being gone is rough and lonely. If he were here, and if he were well, he would grab my hand and take me to the roundhouse at the Seaboard train station where he told me he belonged to the Railway Brotherhood. He had to turn the train around on the tracks. When we studied our 'F' words, I learned about freight locomotives and that Granddaddy had to switch railroad cars from one railroad to another so that the trains would head out of the station in the same direction. I could drink some of that cold water from the iron water fountain and yell something real loud and hear my voice echo like someone was there yelling real loud back to me almost instantly, like a ghost or a voice in the air or something. And as soon as we returned home, the best part was that I could go to Mr. Isenhour's store, on Walkup, where Marshall works, to buy Granddaddy his favorite drink, a Coca- Cola. I might see Marshall at the store.

Daddy Claude was a stout, jolly man who was always smiling about something. He looked like a giant to me. He was the "beautifulest" man I ever knew— even "beautifulier" than Mr. Woods, Mama's insurance man who even Mama, herself, said was a nice looking man. And she doesn't much say things like that unless she is talking about my daddy. Daddy Claude's head was bald and his skin was pinkish brown like the color of the wood kept underneath Grandma's house that she burns in her kitchen stove.

After he had his stroke, Granddaddy couldn't see too *good*, and sometimes I had to be his eyes. I was glad to see for him. That meant my eyes were seeing for two people, which made them twice as important. But one day he surprised me real good. I discovered that he could see a whole lot better than I thought he could. He was about to send me to Mr. Isenhour's store again like he always did in the afternoon after we came home from the railroad station. So he pulled out a coin from his pants pocket held it up and asked me if it was a nickel or a quarter.

I said, "It's a nickel Daddy Claude. Yea, that sure is what it is, all right." All I could think of were those two-for-a-penny Jack coconut cookies that Mr. Isenhour kept in a big jar at his store. So I had to convince him he was giving me a nickel. It was hot and I wanted some cookies and a cup of vanilla ice cream so bad that I planned to eat as I walked home with Granddaddy's bottle of Coke.

He handed it to me to take to the store, and I did just as I had planned. When I returned with Granddaddy's Coke, my hands were some kind of sticky with melted ice cream. I handed the bottle to him. He looked me squarely in the eyes and said, "This bottle's got something mighty sticky on it," Looking at me all the while.

I licked my lips like I do when I'm trying to think of something to say. But this time I licked them to make sure the ice cream and cookie crumbs were all gone, and he wouldn't find any traces of it.

Finally Granddaddy said, "I knew that was a quarter, little girl." He was still eyeing me like the man in the big orange moon in the sky looking down on the ground at night.

I flopped down on the porch without saying a word.

"What did you spend my money on?" Daddy Claude asked.

"Cookies and ice cream," I said in my lowest voice trying not to move my lips, hardly at all.

"It must have been mighty good. It took you long enough to come back here with my drink." he said, and that was the end of it.

But come to think of it, Daddy Claude could have stood giving me a nickel for ice cream and two or three pennies for those two-for-a-penny Jack cookies—he had a *pocket full* of money! Now I'm reminded of what Uncle Horace said about him not helping his grandchildren. Maybe what my uncle said was "*kind of*" true after all. But, I still loved the way he was, and I loved helping him.

Sometimes he did things that I didn't quite understand though—like the times he wanted me to bring him his pee pot. I always brought it whenever I was around and then I would leave the room. After he peed one day, I didn't leave and I saw what happened afterward. I couldn't understand why he was shaking his "thing." I didn't know if I should go and get Grandma to help him or not. I thought of pouring some cold water on it to cool it off. Especially since I thought it might be burning. I didn't know where to turn. So I did go and ask Grandma why it was hot—burning. Mama Allie told me that he was trying to shake the rest of the pee off of it before putting it back into his pants. *That sure was something new to me*.

I remember the very day Granddaddy had his stroke. I had been out riding Aunt Florence's old, half rusted out bicycle, and had just rounded the corner and rode up to the back porch when I heard Mama Allie scream, "Oh Lord Claude's fell out and we can't get him up! Go get your mama! Hurry up! Hurry up!" The ambulance came with a lot of people in white clothes that I had never seen before. They put something like a mask with a hose hooked to it over Granddaddy's face and took him away to what Mama said was Union Memorial Hospital.

The screaming and honking of the ambulance and the red lights flashing lit up the whole neighborhood. Everybody in the nearby houses ran out to see what the matter was. The ladies still wore their kitchen aprons. They all stood around holding on to either their stomachs or their mouths like they were scared to speak, like when you want to answer a question but not sure that you have the right answer.

My mama and Mama Allie rode down to the hospital in Mr. Albert's taxicab. Aunt Florence stayed at the house. They wouldn't let me go with them. Mama said my dress was too dirty for me to go. When the taxicab started up, it sped off out of the yard and right behind the ambulance up the street in the same direction, and I saw my mama and Grandma Allie holding on to the back of Mr. Albert's seat. I ran for a while to the edge of the yard and watched it move out of my sight. Afterwards, I sat on the back porch step for a while where the bicycle was parked just thinking of Daddy Claude and time seemed to stand still. It was late afternoon and still light and some cars were passing by when I sat down, and it was almost dark and no one or nothing in sight when I got up to put the bike away before going inside to ask Aunt Florence about Granddaddy.

It was suppertime, and the good smell of Aunt Florence's golden brown biscuits was drifting from the kitchen onto the porch when I opened the back door. But I couldn't think of eating not even one little bitty bite, not *even* from a biscuit itself that begged for butter and molasses in the middle of it.

Aunt Florence wasn't eating either; she sat in the dining room where Witch and Old Woman hung on the wall, and she almost didn't hear me when I came in and pulled out a chair to sit with her at the table. We just sat there and waited and waited and waited. I finally fell asleep there with my head lying on the table. When

I woke up, my mama was standing there with her hand on my shoulder shaking me, and it was even much later.

I looked into Mama's eyes; she slowly said to Aunt Florence who was standing now, "Daddy had a real bad stroke, and he is going to have to stay in the hospital. Mama has gone to bed."

Aunt Florence stood there quietly listening to what Mama said about Granddaddy without interrupting her. She twisted her hands around and around and twisted her bottom lip underneath the top one and held it there tightly like she wasn't even breathing. It seemed that Aunt Florence twisted her mouth that way so she wouldn't have to show my mama that she was about to cry. But it didn't work because she started crying anyway, and she wiped her eyes with her fingers to keep the water from running down her face onto her neck. Some tears ran to the side and wet her long hair. She wiped them too."Will-he-be-all-right?" She squeezed the words through her tightly held lips. "I mean will he...." She couldn't bring herself to say the words, and Mama took over them for her.

"We don't know what's going to happen. The doctor said we won't know anything until morning. Right now, he's in critical condition in the intensive care unit at the Union Memorial Hospital. The nurses are watching him around the clock."

Aunt Florence finished drying her face, sniffed and flopped down at the dining room table in a chair. My mama stepped close to her and patted her on the back in a loving way like she was patting a baby on the back to make it belch.

"Does Horace know? I mean has he been told?" All of a sudden, Aunt Florence's voice sounded hoarse, I suppose because she had been crying.

Mama answered her, "I haven't seen him. He didn't come by the house today."

I didn't quite know what a stroke was, and I didn't know what critical condition and 'tensive' care was either. So I asked Mama, "Is Granddaddy going to die?"

"I hope not Emilee; we'll just have to wait and see."

It was suppertime, and my stomach started to get that flapjack feeling again. Then I remembered that I hadn't had anything at all to eat since my bologna and biscuit at lunchtime. My stomach sounded like an empty barrel—one that someone dropped something heavy into. It echoed, and Mama heard it and told me to go to the kitchen to get something to eat from the stove.

There were biscuits, fried fatback and Mustard greens in the oven. So I got a bowl from the cupboard and a fork from the drawer and dished out some greens. I put a piece of meat between a biscuit, and brought it back to the table and sat down to eat. I heard the front door open, and it was Uncle Horace coming into the living room. Mama and my aunt went up to meet him, and told him about Granddaddy.

****

Remembering Granddaddy's stroke makes everything I look at around here seem the same way I feel. It's spring and I see leaves on the trees and I see grass; I see birds but they all seem dead to me. I hear a dog barking away down the road like he's calling somebody to bring him something to eat or to come and get him and take him home. He sounds like Frock when he's trying to tell Mama something on Daddy. The wind whips around the trees then whistles. Although it's April, it's chilly, I'm cold and it makes me shiver so that I can hardly hold on to my stick.

Mama Allie must be cooking supper because I smell cornbread. Cornbread: that's a good thought. I take my eyes away from my dirt drawing and a big brown beetle crawls from underneath the step right into the center of the picture I drew of a house with a chimney. I watch him crawl sideways, then in another direction. I put my stick in front of him and watch him change directions again. I take my stick and help push him along, back underneath the step. I'll go and get a jar to put him in and take him home to feed him—take care of him and bring him back tomorrow to make sure nothing happens to him because I'm sure I have enough to worry about, and I'm in enough trouble without having to worry about killing anything else.

Vettie's not home again today. She and her mother have been away from home a lot since her father died. Her mama took her up to the city to her other daughter's house who has that big job up there working for the government in Charlotte according to what Mama said Miss Anna Lee told her. They took the train. Vettie hadn't talked to me in a long time, but the other day she told me they're taking her to Belks to buy her and her brother new clothes for Easter. Mama has already started to cut the newspaper pattern for my Easter dress that she's making me.

I sure do wish my mama would take me up to Charlotte though; I've never been there. I've been to Belks in Morris Town once and I've been to Woolworth lots of times. I went with my sister to Belks when Daddy gave Ruth and me money to buy Mama a new blanket for her birthday. We picked out a pretty, soft blue one for Mama.

I think Charlotte must be a really big city, like a place called New Jersey, where one of my daddy's brother's lives. I don't know that much about Belks. You can't learn much about a place going just one time. But I know all about Sears because Mama Allie ordered some sheets and pillowcases out of her Sears and Roebuck catalogue. A big truck brought them to her in a gigantic box and sat it on the front porch. She had to come to the door and sign a paper that the man who brought it handed her before she could keep the box. After that, they sent her a new book for where to order her sheets, pillowcases and curtains. And she let me cut paper dolls out of her old book. I have a whole box of paper dolls that Aunt Florence and I play with after we eat whenever I have supper with her. Aunt Florence cuts her paper dolls out of the Sunday Charlotte Observer newspaper.

I get up to knock on Mama Allie's door to get a jar for my bug and some cornbread with butter for myself, and of all the luck in the world, that old bug had crawled right near my foot and I squashed him but good. It crawled underneath my red shoe. I peep at the bottom of my shoe, and that bug is flatter than a tin can that's been run over by a train on a railroad track. I sure hope it wasn't a mama or a daddy bug because the little children will be looking for it to come home with some food. But if it wasn't, then it was a baby bug and its mama would surely be looking for it to come home. I take my stick and scrape the bug from the bottom of my shoe. A little speck of grayish white stuff that came out of the bug is still stuck there. I think I had better go on down the path, wash and dry my shoe. It might not be too good for me to let the stuff stay there. That bug might try to come and get me, haunt me tonight when I go to bed.

It seems like every time I get something or someone just for me, something happens—just like my doll with the pretty blue eyes that open and shut that said "Mama"—just like my music box that played "East side, West side".—just like my granddaddy.

My doll's head was torn off, and I found it lying under the bed. I tried to put the head back on it but it wouldn't close its eyes or say mama anymore when I laid her down. My music box wouldn't turn anymore. It's my fault about Granddaddy and this bug, but my dolls and my music box were somebody else's fault. And I know who it is. Although I'm not perfectly sure about it, but I believe my brother, Daniel, had a hand on the doll and the music box. I believe he broke them because he's the one that's all the time trying to see how things work and fit together. And it won't do one bit of good to complain to Mama either because he just tells her he didn't do it and she just lets him slide.

I walk down the path on one foot and one heel and into the house and straight to the bathroom to get a rag to wash off the bottom of my shoe. I take it off and carefully hold my shoe bottom under the running water in the sink.

Daniel comes in wearing his shoes with the cap bottles attached to the heels— click clack, click clack across the room. "Boo!" He makes me jump and I drop my shoe into the sink. The whole shoe gets wet.

I yell at him, "Now look at what you made me do!"

"What are you washing off your shoe for? Why do you have your shoe in the sink? What did you do Emilee? I'm gone tell Mama you got your shoe wet!"

"Never mind, get out of here, Daniel!" I yell.

He runs away, click clack, click clack, click clack, promising, "When I grow up, I'm going to beat you up every day, Emilee!"

What Daniel doesn't realize is I know his words are just an idle threat coming from a little brother. Maybe he feels left out because he's the only boy in the family. Maybe he sometimes feels the way I do when it comes to Mama and Ruth.

Mama is taking a nap right now so I tiptoe through her room to the kitchen and I put my shoe in the oven to dry it fast; then I start my spelling homework. Mrs. Faulkner says spelling is a real important skill. She says you have to spell to write and when you spell words correctly, people see you as a very learned person, and it makes people sit up and notice you.

I can use all of the noticing I can get because Mama loves my sister, Ruth; and Daddy loves Daniel. They have some special kind of language and all. The first thing Daddy says when he comes home after seeing where Mama is, "Where's Daniel?" I wish he would ask for me first just once in his life. I wouldn't know how to act if he did. I did have Granddaddy. Now I have nobody.

I had just finished word number eight when my mama wakes up and rushes in to discover something is burning. "What in the world is that smell? What's in the oven?" She asks then rushes over, yanks open the oven door and a big ball of blue smoke hits her in the face. She jumps back from the smoke to get a dishcloth and pulls out the oven rack. "What in the world?"

And wouldn't you know it? It would have to be my shoe in the oven. It was smoking. When she lifted it up, it was curled up at the toe just like the witch's shoes in the Wizard of Oz.

After my shoe burns, I feel so tired and fall asleep on the sofa in front of the TV. When I awake, Mama, Daddy, Ruth and Daniel are watching the ten o'clock news report of the Morris Town sky burning with the exchange of gunshots.

The reporter says, "Whites chased RW and a carload of Negroes down the highway after they and some Freedom Riders picketed the 'whites only' swimming pool, and when their car was finally forced off the road and came to a stop, white men carrying guns surrounded it. RW and his followers jumped out of his car unexpectedly with their guns, and suddenly gunshots were exchanged which made the Whites run away in fear for their own safety." The news showed one white man, who fell to the ground and cried,

"They have guns—the 'GD niggers' have guns and the police can't even arrest them. Oh Lord, oh Lord; what has this world come to!"

<u>11</u>

With all that happened on the Morris Town streets reported in the news last night, Mama left the TV on I imagined because there was another hour before the station's National Anthem sigh off, and that the noise from the television might keep us from hearing our parents' talk. So the house was quiet. Even Ruth was hushed. I suppose all of us were made more tired than usual after hearing about guns aimed at RW and his followers. Although it was late, Mama told us to prepare for school before going to bed.

It's a good thing I can still wear my shoe that almost burned in the oven. Once it cooled off, the toe felt tight, but it hadn't been completely ruined. It won't be long before I get new ones.

* * * * * * * * *

Today we go about our routine at school, because our teacher keeps us busy and our minds occupied with plenty of school work: science, math, reading, writing, spelling and tests. Today we're up to the 'S' spelling words in Mrs. Faulkner's fifth grade class. I make a 95 on my test. I even beat James. He turns around in his seat and gives me a hard look when Mrs. Faulkner said, "Emilee made a 95 on her test." James made a 92. I made a good grade because I really wanted to. I can do anything when I really put my mind to it. Besides, the first thing I do after we eat supper is start looking up the rest of the 'S' words—superman, supermarket, supervise, and superstition.

Superstition: an unreasonable belief in an omen. Omen: a sign or event of the future.

Superstition: an untrue belief. Mrs. Faulkner explains it and gives an example of a superstition. She says it's an old saying like "step on the crack break your mama's back; point at a graveyard and your finger will fall off."

The first thing that comes to mind is what I ask. "Mrs. Faulkner", I say, "If you wash on New Year's Day, can you wash someone out of the family?" For a few seconds there is silence and then James and some others start to snicker. Then I say, "What I mean to say is, can you cause someone to die?"

Mrs. Faulkner quiets the class. "Well what makes you ask Emilee?" She asks sitting behind her desk.

I shrug my shoulders because I did not want anyone else laughing at me. Then, like magic, Mrs. Faulkner repeats the very words Mama said and almost in the same way Mama said them, but the difference is that it is **untrue**.

She says that this is something made up—an opinion people just go around believing in without really thinking about it, therefore being scared for no reason, like I was going around being scared of causing Daddy Claude's death.

This means that I did not kill my granddaddy. This means I did not wash the life out of him at all. He must have just lay there and died like a lot of old people do, like Aunt Lil's husband, Uncle Will, after living a long time. It was not my fault at all! I
can tell by James and the classmate's reactions to my question. It seems they know better than to believe such a thing. Fifty pounds of worry lifts off my mind. I suddenly feel like I can eat a big lunch and a big supper. I do not have to worry about it anymore. Now instead of having to tell Mama some bad news, I can tell her some good news. This good news about the superstition will relieve her too because she won't have to believe that washing on News Years Day can kill someone either.

Mrs. Faulkner says, and the dictionary might as well have said too, that you cannot wash somebody out of the family. Now that I think of it—it is pretty silly. The thoughts of my granddaddy just dying makes my heart feel like I had been walking with books on top of my head, weighting me down, and suddenly the books fall off. I just can't wait to get home to tell my mama all about what I've learned. All of this information really has started me to thinking and wondering. I mean thinking a lot.

I cannot keep my mind on Mrs. Faulkner's words nor that she's sitting directly in front of us at her desk. I wonder about Miss Mae Lee's daughter, Lois, and her baby. I remember hearing my grandma talking to Lois's mama, Miss Mae Lee, in the kitchen one day. They didn't know I was listening. I was supposed to be getting some wood from under the house from the woodshed for Grandma to burn in the kitchen stove.

Miss Mae Lee told Grandma, "Lois's husband left her the other day. He was mad at her because their baby turned out to be a white baby." Said, "Lois couldn't help it that she had been scared by a white cow."

The back door was open, and just as I started to crawl under the house, I heard Miss Mae Lee say, "You know the old saying, Miss Allie, if you get scared by a white cow, your baby will be born white. And that baby's skin is as white as it can be. It's as white as any white person's, just like the baby that I use to keep for them white folk down the road in Camp Sutter. Now, Allie, I know it don't look nothin like Lois or Jimmy— both of them is dark skinned. But we all know 'bout Lois and that there cow, too. Jimmy was so mad he could have spit nails last night when he left. Seem that some of the boys down there on his job at the bakery were whispering "thangs" bout Lois and old man Brady, the man she works for. Lois tried to soothe him. But that didn't help *none* at all."

It seemed like my grandma and Miss Mae Lee finally discovered that I was listening. But they didn't seem to mind. So I walked up the steps with the wood and piled it up on the back porch and sat down on the step. They kept on talking. I heard Mama Allie say, "Now don't fret so over them grown folks. He'll probably cool off and come back."

Miss Mae Lee continued, "I know one 'thang'. He had better come back. Lois can't take care of them chaps they got all by herself. And you know I'm not able to do it. I'm half dead from working all the time, can't half see and down in my back anyway. What am I gone do if Lois starts back working and leaves them babies home wid me to take care of? He's just got to come back home. That's all there is to it."

I got tired of sitting on the step, so I got up and went inside the kitchen and sat on the chair near the stove. Mama Allie had made a pot of coffee in her silver pot, and she poured Miss Mae Lee a cup of it. Miss Mae Lee sat there stirring in her cup and staring straight ahead for a short while. She made some dry smacking sounds with her lips then she took a sip of her coffee. She held the cup up close to her eyes to see how much coffee she had left before she drank any more. She's right when she says she can't half see, and she probably can't smell either because the middle skin part of her nose is missing too. People who live around Mama Allie's neighborhood said that a rat came right up on her bed one night and bit a plug out of her nose while she lay sleeping.

"Emilee, is that you baby?" She asked. Then she drank some more of her coffee. Before I could answer, she said, "Here, take this here cup for me and put it over yonder in that there sink, honey."

I got up and took the cup to the sink. Miss Mae Lee sat there. She looked all weak like a worn out switch that's been broken from a tree limb and all the green has turned brown. The skin on her face, hands, and legs is all spotted. It seemed she might have been a pretty woman before this happened—before life got to her. But old age got to her right after life did. She lived down the street from where Mama Allie used to live in a little brown shack of a house with her daughter and her daughter's husband and their two children on Seaboard Street.

She told Grandma, "You know, Lois had a good job, doin housework for the whites before she got married to Jimmy. Lois is a pretty and stout girl. And the people she worked for was real crazy bout her." She sucked in her breath and made some more smacking sounds. She started to talk again, "That woman she worked for left the care of her chillums and her husband in Lois's hands whenever she traveled out of town on business and everything, working up there for Southern Electric Company. You know she would be gone sometimes for the whole week. Lois would have to stay over there wid the family all night long. She would even have to drive their car to take them white chaps to school."

I am thinking so hard that I don't hear Mrs. Faulkner call my name to make a sentence with one of the 'S' words--supervise.

I come home from school all excited and ready to tell Mama what I learned about the superstition, that Mrs. Faulkner said it is just an old belief with no value. And I know I had better pick a good time to disagree with Mama, too. Once my mama gets it into her head about an idea, she can be just like old man Hershey's mule; she won't budge for anything unless her life depends on it.

While she's cooking in the kitchen won't be a good time to get her attention because she'll be too busy and have her mind on the dinner she's preparing. So I'll have to watch and see if she's in a good mood later while she's doing her sewing and her needlework.

Right after supper, Ruth goes off to basketball practice so the kitchen is left to me for cleaning. I clean the table real good, wash the dishes and sweep the floor. Mama comes back into the kitchen and I see that she notices the work I've done. She looks over at the table and then at me. She doesn't say anything, but I know by her face that she has given me a sign of approval. But with Mama you never really know whether she's happy or not. She acts so strangely. That's how things are with her, I find myself always struggling for her approval. And, for an instant it is here, I have it, and strangely enough, her approval is only temporary, to be forgotten when the next event comes and she's not satisfied.

Mama's strange actions these days, I believe, are because of the fear. She has good reasons for being afraid: I heard her and Daddy's talking about his dangerous involvement with his cousin RW's Black Armed Guard. He said, "The NAACP members who carry legal weapons, established by the NRA, for self-defense strategies." Mama told Daddy, "Jomis, I fear for our children's lives, and I fear for our jobs."

Negroes and Whites are shooting at each other. And of all things the Whites are calling Negroes "the 'n' word," according to the dictionary, considered, I recently learned, and now I know, is the worst name for a person. I wanted to define the word "nigger," because I wasn't sure of the meaning. I didn't want to ask my parents, they have so much to focus on without my adding this too.

So I looked up several references:
> One reference says: a (noun) describes an ignorant, uneducated, foolish individual, regardless of race, color, religion, sexual orientation, etc.

The Old Oxford Dictionary says:

> The word nigger was first used as an adjective denoting a black person in the 17th century, and has long had strong offensive connotations. Today it remains one of the most racially offensive words in the language.

It's a hurting thing to think that a man like my sweet, sweet, nice; hard-working daddy might be called that nasty 'n' word. I see that Mama's fears are "for real", especially with Daddy involved in RW's Black Armed Guard. I have these same fears. What if Daddy has to carry a gun and someone shoots at him? He could be killed. And what I can't understand is why would someone try to degrade another person for wanting a better life? No wonder Mama is acting strangely.

Just two weeks ago, I thought I had done everything that would get Mama's permission for Uncle Andes daughter, my cousin, Barbara's birthday party. All the classmates were going, and I can walk to Bent Hill. So I cleaned the house, cooked and washed dishes. Then I asked Mama if I could go to Barbara's party at Bent Hill. She didn't hesitate. She told me "NO!" I mentioned the work I had done and that Barbara would have our other cousins at the party too; I started to name just a few of them: Hulet's daughter, Hector's sons and daughters, Ella Rose's girls, Cousin Nate, Aunt Loving's son.

Mama turned and said, "I said No!"

I didn't give up, thinking she might see that I really wanted to go. Mama walked up to me and gave me a smack across my lips. So I know her sign of disapproval can turn *ugly* when it comes to me.

As soon as I finish in the kitchen, I go to the back room, get my spelling book and go to the bedroom where Mama is pedaling her sewing machine. I don't have to worry about Daddy being here and interrupting because he has already gone out into the backyard into the shop to cover Mr. McKane's sofa. He took Daniel with him, and I know they will be out there until real late because Mr. McKane is picking his chairs up on Saturday and Daddy doesn't have a lot of time to finish them. It's already Thursday. He'll send Daniel in to go to bed soon. Daniel will be so tired and sleepy that he'll go straight to bed. So I'll have Mama all to myself.

Anyway, I sit on the foot of Mama's bed with my book. Mama sits at the sewing machine with her back to me. I say, "I made a 95 on my spelling words today Mama."

Without missing a stroke on the sewing machine pedal Mama says, "That's good."

"We had to spell ten's' words," I tell her, and I start calling them off one after another: "Superman, supermarket, supervise." Then I come to the last one, I draw in my breath and I say, "Superstition."

Mama pauses for a second or two. My heart stops. Mama starts to work the pedal of the sewing machine with her feet again, and my heart starts to beat again.

I think I can start with some other superstitions before building up to the main one. "Mama," I say. "My teacher Mrs. Faulkner said that there's no such thing as sweeping your feet and going to jail, or stepping on the crack and breaking your mama's back."

Mama says, "She did. Did she?" And she keeps on pedaling and sewing: Her hands are guiding the material under the needle that bobs up and down; her feet works the sewing-machine pedal back and forth as she sews.

I am determined to get my point across to her. "She said it is silly to think that you can wash somebody out of the family on New Year's Day too."

Then there is complete silence—silence from Mama, silence from the bobbing up and down needle, silence from the pedal, silence in the whole house and silence from me. This is the one time I wish for Daniel to come running in with some unexpected noise, to take Mama's thoughts away from what I have just said. That's always the trouble with Daniel; he's never around when I need him to save me.

Mama turns around and stares me down from my head to my toes for a short while and I feel her penetrating *'matter of factly look.'* And I'm sitting here trying to figure out what she will say and what will happen—what will be my consequences. I'm sitting here wishing that something inside my head had stopped me. *I'm sitting here thinking now that Mama is looking at me and paying me the attention that she hasn't before, and that she might see the pain in my face from missing Daddy Claude, the pain that shows itself even when I'm trying real hard not to let it out,* like the smell of one of her cakes in the oven. You can't see it, but you know it's there because it fills up the whole house. I'm sitting here with this pain filling up my face and my whole body. I can't move. I hold onto my book tightly.

It's not often when Mama is searching for words. She twists her mouth around like she is trying to let some words out and keep some of them in.

She finally speaks. "I suspect you trying to tell me that your teacher knows everything. Is that right?"

I'm not sure if I should answer or not—but I do. "No Mama," I say.

"Well she **don't** know everything! She **don't**. You hear me?! She can't tell me about what my family believes in. You understand me girl? Now get out of here with that nonsense and go to bed and let me get back to my sewing!"

I do as I'm told. I do completely understand the double edge sword, which disturbs Mama, and the town Negroes would surely be empathetic. Mama's unhappiness more aims at Daddy than with my attempt to question the family's old and unfounded beliefs. Inside my heart as well as my head, I know Mama's anger derives from panic. She holds the fear like most of the Black women whose husbands or fathers have any involvement with the Black Armed Guard formed by RW in Morris Town to defend the Negroes from KKK activities—night raids in Negro communities, death threats and bombing threats toward them.

Mrs. Faulkner had us read about it in the Morris Town Newspaper. It said that the "newly formed organization needed veterans who knew about weaponry and ammunition, and who were unafraid to defend their families against the hooded terrorists."

I heard Daddy tell Mama, "RW and his advocate, the local black physician Dr. Phelps called upon his Army World War II expertise with weaponry repair."

I know this troubled Mama tremendously. They spent nights arguing about the dangers involved.

Mama told Daddy, "It's especially dangerous now with the police putting the demonstrating Freedom Riders in jail for fighting for equality, and what's even worse, now there is talk of Dr. Phelps' house being blown up by the Klan following the exchanges of gunfire by whites and Negroes. Jomis, his house is right down the street."

Daddy said, "RW attempt to integrate the "whites only" swimming pool at the Morris Town Country Club caused the whites to get mad."

"All hell has broken lose it seems, and we cannot stop any of it!" Mama told Daddy.

I know my attitude causes Mama to wonder: How will I eventually turn out, Mama thinks I'm different from my sister, Ruth, who she believes only works and plays basketball—Mama thinks Ruth is more like her—Mama works and sews, but I know I am like my daddy, inquisitive, outspoken and defiant at times, yet silent and observant at others. Mama fears Daddy's decision to help his cousin RW could cause both of them to lose their jobs working for the white man.

" Most of all, the trouble between the Whites and Coloreds could cause you to lose your life, and the Morris Town police officers are doing nothing to help the situation, in fact they are part of the problem—the mob themselves." Mama said with Daddy listening.

"The Negroes knew full and well of RW intentions. For instance, if it were not for his defense, two little innocent Negro boys a short while before, one of whom was allegedly kissed by a little white girl in a game; they were about to spend the rest of their lives in Morrison Training School or worst--hung." She further argued, "Warrants labeled the incident an assault on white females. The two boys punished for the *idea* that they could even attempt to play a childhood game with a white girl. However, RW was not about to allow such an unjust punishment."

"If there hadn't been for the national attention brought to the case by RW going on national media to shamed the officials into setting the two boys free, they would have been lynched—two little innocent children our own son, Daniel's age." I heard Daddy tell Mama.

While listening to their argument, I thought about what the television news report said, "Trying to get Whites to swim with Coloreds in a swimming pool is something very similar—the two racial groups mixing in the same water—Whites swimming with what they termed "unfit" Coloreds certainly would defy the Separate but Equal Jim Crow laws of the sixties."

I thought about my talking to Marshall—would this be defiance of the Jim Crow law?

"All together from freeing two little innocent boys for something they allegedly did to providing clean water for little Negro children to swim in pertained to the right and proper thing in terms of justice." Daddy said. "But we know the KKK won't see it that way."

Mama repeated what Miss Anna Lee told Miss Burler when the three of them sat on Mama Allie's porch, "The Morris Town Newspaper reported that some of the major town authorities said, by picketing the swimming pool, RW was not soliciting a swim; he was asking to meet his '*Maker*.' After all when the news spread over town about the two little boys, lynch mobs and shotgun toting Whites sped to the parents' homes in search of the boys and the parents."

Mama added, "I do not want to witness another episode of the same. Whites would fear: first the swimming pool; then what next, entering the front doors of restaurants—sitting in the front seats on trains and busses—integration of our schools—marrying our good white women."

12

I knew it was coming just as sure as my name that Mama would have a talk with my sister, Ruth, about me because she said she's fed up with my smart mouth and my know-it-all attitude, especially after my determination to tell her about superstition. I just can't understand why she didn't talk to Daddy since I'm his daughter and not Ruth's.

There they are sitting in Mama's room on her bed with their heads together as thick as thieves when I get home from school today. So it is no surprise to me.

I don't even let on that I see them. I keep right on walking straight from the front door into the kitchen to the stove to see what is there to eat for supper.

As I stand here, chewing on a biscuit and drinking some sweet water a strong sad feeling comes over me. Even the taste of the sweet water can't take it away. It's empty sadness, a feeling of knowing how close my mama and my sister are; how far away I am from them. They are just two good red apples in a barrel and I guess I must be the rotten one with the brown spot on it about to spoil all of the others.

My mama thinks Ruth can do no wrong. I've seen this happening over and over. How Ruth can manage to keep fooling Mama that she's Miss Perfect, I'll never know. I should tell Mama that she dropped her nail polish into the beans and had to throw the whole pot away. I should tell Mama why she dropped the nail polish too—that same boy from her class that she was kissing was calling her at the kitchen window. It was that old stupid looking Jacob Rushing, again, the one that's always wearing sunglasses at nighttime. Who ever heard of anybody wearing shades at night unless he is as blind as Ray Charles or somebody like Little Stevie Wonder? I do not hate Ruth; I love her. But Mama is making it so difficult not to tell on her, especially when she makes it seem as though I'm the only bad one around here.

Anyway, of all the people Mama decides to talk to about me, it would be her just because I got into a little scrap at school with Mattie Elaine yesterday in the girls' bathroom. Thanks to my sister, now I'm sure

Mama knows all about it. But I couldn't let Mattie Elaine just walk all over me. I wish, just for once I could get away with something—**anything-** without being found out.

I do remember once Daddy and I almost pulled the wool over Mama's eyes though. Daddy let me get on my knees under the steering wheel to drive the car. He operated the gas pedal and the breaks while I drove. He let me turn the corner and everything when we went to the store. I wanted to change the gear, but he wouldn't let me do that.

Daddy and I had a ball. We didn't just go to the store like Mama thought we would. We road all over town, over bumpy roads and hillsides down through the country over by the drive-in movie theater where only the white people can go and Bent Hill where Daddy's people lives. We knew Mama was surely going to have a fit if she was to ever find out about it. I knew I sure didn't want to be around when she did.

Daddy can be some kind of fun at times; whenever he does what he calls "sneaking off." And Frock didn't warn Mama either, because Daddy and I had the good sense to take him along with us for the ride. It seems like Frock had just as much fun as we did. The car window was open, and he leaned his nose out to sniff the air. His two pointed ears sometimes changed directions by the force of the wind. When he became tired of standing, he sat beside Daddy, gazing out at the countryside. Frock stuck his tongue out, and I believe his mouth stayed open the whole time. They say a dog is happy when it does that. Frock must have been some kind of happy. It seems that it does Daddy a world of good to try and get away with something just like it does me. And Frock is just the same.

The only thing, though, is that Daddy doesn't get much time to have fun because he's working almost all of the time. If he's not working up the Charlotte Highway at Mr. Sanford's, he's sure to be out in that old shop he built in the back yard that's piled so high with other folks ragged chairs and sofas, he can hardly get to his power sewing machine.

The only other thing I like almost as much as driving is that every once in a while, Daddy'll let me lather his face with his lather mop. I love to twirl it around in the water and rub it back and forth on the Ivory soap bar to get it all soapy. The soap reminds me of snow cream we make with Pet milk, Vanilla flavoring and sugar after a heavy snow. Then he lets me shave him with his razor while he sits there in a chair. Afterwards, I put some water on his hair and comb it. My daddy's hair is black, shiny like coal and straight— what Mama says people around here call "good hair." So I can put water on it instead of hair grease. Mama gets me to scratch the dandruff off her scalp all the time, but I would much rather comb Daddy's hair anytime than to scratch Mama's head.

Daddy showed me how to take the razor blade and trim his mustache too. He said I've got real steady hands and all. To trim his mustache, he has to tuck in his lips and hold them tightly so I won't cut him with the razor. He never goes to the barbershop because Mama cuts his hair and Daniel's hair too.

My daddy looks real handsome with his yellow skin that shines like the peel of a yellow apple. His lips and nose reminds me of some of the men in the movies—men like Cary Grant. And he's a quiet, and gentle, man. The quietest, gentle, man I know, as gentle as leaves carried by the wind that fall onto the ground.

At first, Mama couldn't figure out what took us so long just to go to the store to get a loaf of bread. She didn't give us a whole list of stuff to get—beans, sugar, bologna, flour and cornmeal --her usual list. When she found out; he had to tell her for some reason—I suppose to keep the peace, as he says. Anyway I thought she was going to put up some kind of fussing at us. But she sure did surprise both of us. She just gave us a long hard look and walked away.

I can tell when Mama is totally outdone by Daddy about a thing because she usually has plenty to say on every given subject, I don't care what it is. But when she's been gotten around by something, she's at a loss for words. It sure doesn't happen often. Since Daddy and I knew we had outdone her, we both grinned at each other behind Mama's back.

But I know I won't be allowed any slack about this fight I had with Mattie Elaine, even if she did start it. She had no business teasing me about never having been kissed by a boy. I told her she didn't know who's kissed me. So she asked me, "Then, who?" I wouldn't tell her that my cousin, Barbara, from the Hill and I used to hide in her father, Uncle Andes's upholstery shop and talk about boys all the time. We used to fix our lips just like the ladies on television right before a man was about to kiss them.

At Ronda Budd's birthday party last summer, we played Spin-the-Bottle. I was hoping to be kissed, but the bottle never stopped on me. I was sort of glad since none of the really cute boys from school was there except for Billy, who's kind of cute. It seemed each time it was Billy Woods' turn he tried to make the bottle land on me. I sure didn't want to get kissed by the school bully and have him brag and tease me about it. Knowing him he would have tried to stick his tongue in my mouth. Yuk!

Right after we got our television set, I used to act like those TV ladies all the time. I would pretend I was kissing someone, just in case I ever got a chance to do it for real. So just because I've never really, really kissed one doesn't mean that I don't know anything about it.

I could have told Mattie Elaine that Marshall, the white boy at Mr. Isenhour's store is fifteen years old, and he sure smiled at me like he might try and kiss me sometime. I suppose that would have run her pure crazy with jealousy. Instead I told Mattie Elaine, "I know plenty about kissing. I probably know more than you do." She got mad and pushed me, and I pushed her back. And she pushed me again—this time twice as hard. Well, the next thing I knew, we were pulling each other's hair and Barbara and the other girls were screaming and pulling us apart.

They got us separated just in time before the bell rang to go back to class. It is a good thing that we both sit on opposite sides in the classroom, or I believe we would have gotten into it again sitting close to each other.

Mattie Elaine was still huffing and puffing in her seat in class. She's sort of fat, and it doesn't take a whole lot to make her work up a good wet sweat. She was just about wringing wet afterwards. She looked like a little fat pig caught up in a rainstorm. She kept on rolling her eyes across the room at me and wiping her face, the back of her neck and around the edges of her hair with a big ball of bathroom toilet tissue, which stuck to the edges of her face.

It's a good thing, too, that we had a math test to concentrate on that was long and hard enough to cool us off and last until school was out.

The news about the fight didn't get to Mrs. Faulkner so we weren't sent to the principal, Mr. Charles' office. It would have meant big trouble had he found out. He would have pulled out that big thick brown leather strap he keeps in the office and given us five hard licks in the hand for fighting. Mr. Charles is big and tall, and he can hit like lighting. You can tell yourself you won't cry. But that leather strap coming down on your hand will make water come from anybody's eyes.

After the test when the dismissal bell rang, neither one of us spoke to each other. We just picked up our books and left without looking at each other at all. I was scared she might try to get me after school because she was always trying to bully the girls around, especially me, because she was fat and I was small. I don't think she expected me to stand up to her. I kind of surprised myself too, especially since I've never been in a fight before. It seems like Mattie Elaine doesn't know how to make friends. She ought to know that you don't get people to like you by picking on them and trying to push them around.

If Mrs. Faulkner didn't hear about the fight, and the principal wasn't told; now I'm wondering, who told my sister? Somebody blabbed to her, and she comes to blab to Mama. Anyway, I am just about to swallow my last piece of biscuit when Mama moves into the kitchen. I know she is going to light into me like pouring kerosene on flames. So I swallow quickly and hold my breath standing at attention like a soldier waiting for his orders.

"Emilee, I know all about the fight at school yesterday." Before I have a chance to respond, Mama's attention is taken away by Mrs. Anna Lee calling her from outside.

Mrs. Anna Lee calls, "What cha doin Martha?"

I supposed Miss Anna Lee wants to sit on the porch and share some more of her, Miss Burla, and the town's gossip.

Before Mama turns to answer her, she says to me, "We'll talk about this later." She shows her pretty, even pearly teeth surrounded by smooth but moist dark brown skin as he goes out the door to answer Mrs. Anna Lee's call.

Green

****

I don't know how I end up seven miles from the house so quickly at Richardson Creek in the late afternoon. I just know I have to get away from everybody and everything. If I run into the Freedom Riders somewhere, I plan to hide on the bus and go with them to New York. So I just keep pedaling, pedaling, riding and riding Aunt Florence's old rusty bicycle, a bicycle she never did come right out and say I could have, even if she is too fat and clumsy to ride anymore, a bicycle she'd had since she was a young girl, I suppose when she was younger than me. The bicycle needs me to give it some life. Otherwise, it would just sit there like her, the way she sits there beside the heater. I never did come right out and ask her if I could have the bicycle either. I felt as long as it was there and I could ride it, then I didn't need to ask her if I could have it. Aunt Florence is a good one for holding on to things that don't matter anymore to her. I can tell they don't matter, because all she does is sit in the house in a chair over in the corner by the oil heater at Mama Allie's and watch TV or stare into space. She sits there with her hair curled; her fingernails polished, and her lips painted with red lipstick. It's like she's waiting on something to happen or someone to show up unexpectedly to take her away—maybe her knight in shining armor.

Aunt Florence had one command. She'd say, "You have that bicycle back here before dark." Then she'd walk away to sit in her spot in the corner. She never gave me a chance to respond, to challenge the command. I supposed she felt I had no rights to the blue bicycle that had more rust than paint on it. It's a girl's bicycle, and to stop it I have to put on brakes, and then I have to jump off the seat and let one foot drag the ground until I come to a halt. My legs aren't long enough to stop it otherwise. And oftentimes while jumping off the seat the bars in the middle bump my body in a way that pains, and sometimes the pain makes me want to burst into sobs, but I never do nor tell anybody. I don't want to seem like a crybaby and a whiner. I'm like my Aunt Florence in a way. She won't talk much and she's got short legs too. Sometimes I wonder if God liked either one of us. And I don't think He did like either one of us because He made us too little—too little to notice, too little to fight back, too little to say much. There's not much that I can reach without sanding on a chair or something.

Now all of a sudden it's like a light comes on in my head with an idea that I never thought of before. I think, maybe that's the reason Mama and Ruth don't like me. I'm not like either one of them. Now I'm mad, well maybe more **sad** than mad, because I never realized until now how much I'm like Aunt Florence. And all the time I've been going around thinking I'm like my daddy. The only thing I have of his is his color and his hair. It seems that I have more of Aunt Florence than of him. This makes my heart pain. I don't want to be like her—someone people don't expect to speak up. No! I refuse to be like her. I think maybe that's why I call Ruth "Archibald." It's such an ugly name. I call her "that awful, ugly name" because I want to let her and Christine know that I'm not going down without a fight—a fight to be noticed, a fight to belong.

Anyway, I just keep going, trying to get away from Ruth and Christine, Aunt Florence, and Mama Allie and the whole bunch. While I ride I'm passing through most of my worries—Daddy Claude's dying, the disappearance of my socks, Ruth and of course Mama— yes Mama, who won't let me explain a dog-gone thing to her. I suddenly remember that I need to get away from Daddy and his love for Daniel too. All the summer months, I spent helping Daddy in the shop while Daniel played. I picked up tacks off the floor, and handed him his tack hammer, and tacked fabric onto chairs, and tied down box springs in chairs, took tacks out of his shoes so they wouldn't stick his feet, and even dumped the ashes off his cigarettes and brought him water. And it was "Emilee, do this", and "Emilee, do that". Yet he always asks about Daniel. I didn't mind too much because at least I was with my daddy, and sharing something. The one I hate to leave, the **only** one I hate leaving is Frock. The two of us are in the same boat. We don't have anybody, and he's tied up outside all alone, and I'm all tied up inside and all alone.

I don't notice the landscape I am passing, or the dangerous curve rounding to the creek. The next thing I know, it's dark all around me and I don't know where I am or the path back home. I get off the bicycle and began walking. I listen to the creaking sounds; I am afraid. In the back of my mind all I can see is the face of Witch and the face of Old Woman celebrating over my being lost and leading me deeper into the woods closer to the water at Richardson Creek. I don't see a single car on the road.

Then out of nowhere, a car rounds the curve and I walk as far from the edge of the road as I can. I start running with the bicycle and duck down beside a tree, almost in tears and too scared to look. Suddenly I hear a car horn honk several times at me, and I know I'm seen; it makes me tremble. I think it must be one of the Ku Klux Klan -Jim Crow coming after me trying to pick me up. I know how mean and dangerous Jim Crow can be, and I remember how they don't think one little thing about killing children. I'm struck with panic in my heart so much that I can hardly breathe, as I turn my head slowly to have a quick look. I see a big white car, and I clearly hear my name being called by a woman whose voice I think sounds familiar.

"Emilee, Emilee, is that you? Where are you going?"

I look up and see that it's Mrs. Isenhour in her big, as Mama says, white Cadillac. I can release my breath.

She is yelling from the car window, "Are you lost, Emilee?" She pulls the car off the road and over near where I'm squatting behind the tree. She stops her car; gets out, without wasting any time; she springs into action. She opens the trunk of the car, trying to put the bicycle inside. It won't fit, so she says, "Leave it over there beside the tree. Marshall will have to come in the truck tomorrow morning to pick it up. It should be all right for tonight. Come on; let's get in the car."

Without hesitation I climb into the front seat of the soft leather and close the car door. I know Mrs.

Isenhour is a nice, kind woman, so I don't have to worry about her knowing Jim Crow or harming me.

Mrs. Isenhour starts the car up, turns it around and pulls off in the opposite direction. She sat behind the wheel with her blond hair gleaming and her diamonds sparkling; her perfume has filled the insides.

"What are you doing out here alone on this dark road? It's much too dangerous for you to be riding a bicycle this far away from home. Did you lose your way?"

"I got lost." I say shyly; clearing my throat and trying to hide tears.

"I thought so. Well, let's get you home. I'm sure your parents are very worried about you about now." She says. Then, "You poor girl, you're trembling."

If it wasn't for her coming along when she did, I don't know what in the world I would have done. Her kindness fills my heart. I know she has a daughter because Mama made a dress for her. But I only see Mrs. Isenhour on occasions in Reverend Isenhour's, her husband's store. I'm enjoying the fuss she's making over me. As we ride along on the way home, I'm lost in thought wondering what it would be like to be *her* daughter. I know the privileges her daughter has that I don't have: eat at the Woolworth counter, buy a hamburger and ice cream sundae at the front door of Ten Points, swim and attend parties in the Country Club swimming pool. It doesn't seem that Mrs. Isenhour is thinking of or worried about any dangers for taking me home.

Mrs. Isenhour pulls her car up in front of our house on Fairley. She opens the car door, gets out and walks with me up to the porch.

Mama is looking out of the window and when she sees Mrs. Isenhour, she opens the door. "Emilee, where in the world have you been?"

Before I can answer, Mrs. Isenhour says, "I picked this child up on Roosevelt Boulevard near Richardson Creek riding her bicycle. We had to leave the bike—it was too big for the trunk. But don't worry; I'll have Marshall pick it up in the morning. It should be all right for tonight. It shouldn't be that much traffic on the road before then." Then she turns to return to the car. "Good night." She climbs into the car.

Mama yells, "Thank you for bringing her home."

We hear Mrs. Isenhour crank up the car; we watch her drive away.

"Come on in here, Emilee. I don't know what you were thinking, disappearing and riding that dog gone bicycle that far away from home. I was worried sick. You *know* it's too dangerous for you to be out by yourself with everything that's going on around here. You had better be glad your daddy is still at work, or he would have torn this town up looking for you in that Buick."

I do as I am told and walk stiffly into the house.

Then Mama turns the whole conversation around. She says, "Why didn't you tell me? You didn't let that old girl, from down yonder pick on you and push you round—good for you. I know from my own past school experiences, sometimes a girl has to fight for whatever reason. In my school days with your daddy, I've had to "smack a girl down" on occasions because of some petty incident—usually about some girl's jealousy over Jomis' dating me instead of her."

Once again I can breathe. My stiffness changes and I see Mama's eyes. I see they are soft and look happy to see me, and I can tell she's really not mad at me for defending myself. I also see that *Mama and I agree, for the first time, on this matter*—for both of us are like our cousin, RW, and the way the locals say, he is: *standing up for self defense, self-respect, and self-determination.*

I surely didn't want to come home and have to fight with Mama after fighting with Mattie Elaine and then getting lost. I feel like a limp dishrag. Mama touches my arm, curls her long slim fingers around it and gives it a little delicate squeeze. She turns and walks away.

Mama has to worry about bigger matters. Later that night we watched the television set when the reporters were rehashing the same issues of when RW took a carload of Coloreds over to the Morris Town

"Whites only", Country Club swimming pool, that he did it because he wants to agitate the whole community into an uproar. The mayor of the city and the police chief has decided to close the swimming pool and cement it up to keep this from happening. Then suddenly in the middle of the report there is an emergency alert: The reporter says, "We have **AN ALL POINTS BULLETIN!**"

These words flash across the screen. Daddy shifts to the edge of the sofa; Mama folds her arms across her chest. We all watch as the police chief says, "At approximately eight-thirty this evening, this man, six foot three, two-hundred and twenty pound, Negro male, (a picture of RW is shown on the screen), RW, a Civil Rights activists, and president of the NAACP here in Morris Town, was charged with kidnapping a white couple who road through the Colored neighborhood on Tobye Street where RW lives." (A camera shows RW's home). "He kept the couple hostage for hours before later allowing them to leave. Now, the search by the Morris Town police and the State Highway Patrol is in progress for RW, his wife Mabelle, and their two sons at the home on Tobye Street have been unsuccessful and the FBI has listed him as **Wanted, Armed and Dangerous**." Then an **UPDATE** on television appears: "Authorities believed that RW has left the state and perhaps the country—he and his whole family. The streets are swarming with police cars everywhere in search of them."

I see deep lines form across Daddy's forehead. Finally he says, "*My God*. I hope they're all right. And I hope they're somewhere safe. Those poor little sons of his have had to leave their home. I know RW would not kidnap anyone. I don't care what the newsman says. I know better than to believe that. I just don't believe that."

Mama and the rest of us are silent; I suppose she is searching for words. If the police are everywhere, I'm thinking, we just may not have to go to school tomorrow. Then I'm also thinking, how awful it might have turned out if Mrs. Isenhour hadn't come along when she did or I might have been shot right out there on Roosevelt Boulevard.

Ruth added quietly with emotions, "I know Mabelle must be terrified."

<u>13</u>

It seems like we are walking on egg shells at home and at school in the days that follow RW and his family's disappearance. We go to school, but are careful not to talk about what happened. Besides if asked, I imagine Ruth might know how because of her older classmates, but I wouldn't know how to explain our cousin's disappearance.

My brother Daniel is his mischievous self. I thought he was with Daddy in the shotgun upholstery shop helping with something; then I find out for sure he wasn't. If it hadn't been for him, the one who's never around when *I* need him to *save* me, if it wasn't for him digging a hole to bury that stinking dead frog, my socks would still be where I hid them, and Mama and me would still be buddy-buddy. **But No!** He had to find them right at the time when Mama is feeling proud of me for standing up against Mattie Elaine at Winchester School and for having me safely at home.

Of all the places in the back yard to dig a hole, he had to dig one at the Pecan tree in the very same spot where my socks were buried. Knowing Daniel, I am sure, the only way this could possibly have happened. He must have been somewhere hiding and peeping when I laid the last handful of dirt over them. It would be just like Daniel to be sneaking around watching to see what I'm doing so he can spoil everything. I don't know which one of them is worse, Ruth or him.

He's about to cause a big uproar in the house. It's not enough that RW has Mama and Daddy in confusion over what the news said about him and his family missing. The lights in the kitchen just about stay on all night, and they have been up half the night,
drinking coffee. I heard them talking about how the police and the FBI are trying to find them. **And now Mama has to start thinking about Daddy Claude dying all over again.**

So of all things, Daniel comes running in the house dangling those green socks on a stick and shouting like he has struck gold. I'm sitting on the sofa getting ready to start on my spelling homework when Daniel runs pass me.

"Mama, look at what I found buried in a hole in the back yard. Aren't these Emilee's green socks?" he yells.

Mama is in the kitchen making supper when he comes running in. She is standing over the stove. I see her look up, turn around, wipe her hands on a dishtowel and take a closer look. After a closer examination, she questions Daniel. "Boy what in the world are you doing with those dirty socks?" To make sure that she is seeing right, Mama calls me to the kitchen. "Em-i-lee, come in here." She calls in the most serious voice that I think I have ever heard.

Anytime she says my name in three separate parts, I know I need to stiffen up because it'll be like when Rickey Ricardo told his wife, Lucy, "You got some serious 'splaining' to do." I begin to run my story over in my mind—everything—the evidence for the account I'm going to tell Mama.

I put my homework down on the sofa. We're up to the Vs for vicious brother or victim in my case. With sheer dread and chills running up the back of my neck, I go to the kitchen to answer Mama's call. I can't get my legs to move any faster since they don't want to go anyway, so it takes me some time to get there.

Daniel, the vengeful devil, stands there in the middle of the kitchen floor with the green socks covered with dirt still dangling on a stick. The grin on his face tells me that he is more than proud of his work—to have been the discoverer. I guess he feels like Christopher Columbus given credit for finding the new world except that he is about to cause my world to come tumbling down around me.

I freeze when I see the green socks right before me because I know now that I have to do what Perry Mason on TV would make people do on the witness stand referred to as "Tell the truth, the whole truth and nothing but the truth so help me God." I know now that my mother is going to make the connection between, my grandfather's death, and what I was trying to explain about superstition, when she became upset and made me go to bed the last time that I talked to her about school. I had failed to make her understand at my last attempt to get myself off the hook for Granddaddy's death.

I give my brother a real hard *why did you have to go and do this* look, and he sticks his tongue out at me and sits down in a chair to wait out the what's going to happen now question.

Mama begins, "Emilee, are those your socks, the ones you said you couldn't find? The ones I washed, rolled and put on your bed?"

I think to myself**, now she knows they're mine**! I'm glad she at least asked me if they're mine. It gives me time to think. I think maybe this won't be as bad as it seems. Maybe Mama will feel sorry for me after all. I am very tempted to lie, but I know the Lord is watching me, so I do not attempt it, knowing I might make Him bring the "wrath" down on me that Reverend Little preached about: He said, "A stone is heavy, and sand weighty, but a fool's wrath is heavier than the both of them." I surely don't want to be a fool—walking around with more weight on my mind than I already have. So I answer truthfully, but diplomatically, (remembering our spelling word, diplomatically) "Yes Mama," I say, "They **look** like the ones I used to have."

Daniel starts to laugh and says, "That's a good one, Emilee."

Mama gives him a, you had better stop look, and he swallows his laugh. She tells him, "Take the socks and put them in the washing machine." Daniel goes to the back room where the washing machine sits.

Then Mama folds her arms across her chest. "Now what do you mean they look like the ones you use to have? Are-those-your-socks-or-are-they-not-your-socks?" Her question sends another chill over me by the manner of how she asked.

"Yes mama, they're mine." I get myself ready now for the next question that I know is coming.
"What were your socks doing buried in the back yard? And you had better have a good reason." She stands here with her arms still folded and waiting for me to speak.

Mama can be the most direct person in the world when she means business. No beating around the bush here—not today. She is out for blood—mine.

"Em-i-lee I asked you, what were your good socks doing buried in the back yard?"

Now suddenly the green socks have become the *good* green socks. I stand here wondering how I can

begin to tell all that happened. What am I going to do?
I know I am going to get a killing. Perhaps tears are my
only saving-grace. So I think I will at least try it. I start
to cry. I soon see; Mama isn't going for it. She is
persistent.

"Are you planning to answer or do you plan to
wait until I put my belt to your butt?"Mama sits down
at the table directly across from where I stand and folds
her hands and looks at me with a, this had better be
good look. "I'm getting tired of waiting, Emilee."

"Mama," I began. "I buried the socks because..."
Then I change the direction of my explanation. I
nervously began jittering my feet and waving my arms
and speaking hurriedly, "I mean, do you remember
when I made a 95 on my spelling words and I told you
about Mrs. Faulkner telling us about Webster and the
word *superstition*?"

Mama suddenly shrieks, "What in the world does
that have to do with your socks being buried in the back
yard, girl? And I'm not going to wait much longer for
you to explain yourself either."

I become scared and blurt out in tears what I
don't mean to say. "I washed my socks on New Year's
Day because my white ones were dirty, and I couldn't
find my other pair." I continue really bawling now. "I
forgot about washing somebody out of the family,
Mama. And when Granddaddy died, I didn't want
anybody to find out. But Mama, Mrs. Faulkner said you
can't cause somebody to die by washing something." I
say this too, without thinking.

At first Mama is still sitting at the kitchen table, but when I bring up the subject of superstition and Mrs. Faulkner, it seems that Mama suddenly remembers everything from before, especially about my calling her beliefs silly. I seem to bring up my mama's childhood memories and the whole family's painful secrets and important matters of life and death.

Mama stands; she begins, **"So-you-washed-your-socks-on-New-Year's-Day?"**

The question at once completely gets the best of me. I wished like crazy that I could make myself invisible and disappear right before her eyes. I think maybe disappear like RW and his family. But since I can't disappear, I try to faint. I heard that if you hold your breath and push your knees together real hard, you can pass out. I do this but I can't faint either. I can't say a word. I just stand here with two big white eyes about to pop out of my face. My anticipation of Mama's actions seems to take hours and take on its very own meaning. This whole event is too centered with how Mama might act when she finds out about Daddy Claude, the idea that he would still be alive and here with us if it wasn't for me. For the second time that I can remember, I wish for Daniel to return to the kitchen so that some silly actions of his could get Mama's attention onto him. I view what is happening now as my own fault for failing at running away—*for not getting out and staying out while the getting out was good*, while Mama had good thoughts about me. I knew all along, the whole event would come crashing down on my head. But I got caught up in thinking my secret was safe as long as the evidence was buried in the back yard. So I kind of thought I had nothing to worry about.

At first Mama's look is mad and mean as if she can't trust me. Then suddenly as the lightening stops, the clouds move and the sun appears, she seems to turn all of her thoughts to a gentler and softer side—I could hear hurt in her voice, and I could see it in her eyes. She simply says, "***Never mind***." She seems to stare at my eyes as she is seeing herself or at least her own daughter terrified and sorry. Mama seems to be me for the first time, and I seem to be her. Never mind. **Never mind is all she says?**

I want to cry for the pain so visible in her face. I want to cry that she thinks I do not feel the pain she feels about her beliefs and that she wants them respected. I want to cry because Mama's life represents the ***old*** way of living. And now she has lost touch because of the new generation like me—young people who listen to teachers in school who teach us to think for ourselves, young people who read books, look up words and then come running home trying to change everything older people like my mother clings to and make them feel they don't belong anymore. I could sense all this and more in my mother's eyes. Her look at me now seems to say, ***what am I going to do with her***? As we stand here gazing at each other, Mama doesn't speak another word. She turns, and walks to the kitchen sink to complete dinner. She begins humming, "Like a Bridge Over Troubled Waters." I don't know if this ordeal is over or not, but after a moment, I too turn and leave the room. I whisper to her in my mind, **"I'm sorry Mama."**

I believe the hurt in Mama's face and her silence was more painful than if she had backhanded me, causing me to see stars.

14

    Thank goodness the sock mystery thing is over, as Mama Allie would say, 'over and done with.' Burying them in the dirt under the Pecan tree caused them to be ruin, and the washing machine finished them off for good. If they hadn't been ruined, I just couldn't bring myself to wear them again. Somehow they symbolized Granddaddy's death. When we studied the 'S' words, Mrs. Faulkner taught us about symbolic images. When one thing represents another, she says like a dove representing peace. Having those socks out of the way sure have created more peace in this family. I believe Mama's words, 'Never Mind' sounded just like sweet water tastes.

In the hearts of the townspeople it is known that the Freedom Riders' bus rode out of Morris Town. The swimming pool was cemented up. According to the report on the black and white TV, RW his wife and family left everything they owned and fled during the night in exile to Canada, then Cuba with Fidel Castro to start life over.

The townspeople buzz with news of how it all came down. The residents of the communities continue their previously held jobs: upholstery small business; Hersey's Grill; small market owners; janitors, painters, hospital workers, housekeepers, construction workers, barber shop owners, beauty parlor owners, and shade tree mechanics, railroad workers, numerous teachers, doctors, and lawyers. When I grow up, I think I might matriculate to Shaw University, in Raleigh, where Daddy attended, and become a teacher like Mrs. Faulkner. Mrs. Faulkner had us research each one of these jobs for our future goals. From the neighborhood talk, some believe their lives were affected either positively or negatively, but the main focus and belief are how the Ku Klux Klan raids came to an abrupt halt because of RW's effort to instill the ideology of self defense and self respect for men—black men and women.

According to what Daddy says, "The townspeople know that although there is an outwardly air of quietness in the town, there is still an underlying uneasiness in the surroundings among its people. RW is absent, but what is also absent is the hope for change— some type of equality, some hope for dignity, some relief of back door entrances, some changing of the guard for separate facilities, home before dark activities, safe, warm swimming facilities."

May is like no other month. It has turned out to be a happy time again—when families pushing baby strollers take long walks through neighborhoods down Winchester and over the Overhead Bridge that runs above the Seaboard Railroad tracks where Daddy Claude worked before he died. The bridge leads downtown onto Church Street. We often walk in the evening when there is a warm breeze blowing and when the sun, after shining brightly during the day, completes its work and goes down.

Sometimes the grown folks just sit out on the front porch until dark to watch the sky in search of the Big Dipper, the Little Dipper and the North Star, in a laid-back manner. Some take their brown fingers that have become powder white from digging into the Argo starch box and pick out the largest chunks to chew on, or they spit out snuff and share their versions of the goings on of the day. But if you're young, the best ways to spend the evening is to lie flat on the ground, on your back, look straight up, watch the sky and become consumed by the heavens now that the danger of the hooded men riding in our neighborhoods has gone.

Miss Anna Lee's porch is directly across the street from ours, and supported by red bricks and so high up off the ground that you can see all the trash underneath it, an old tire, broom handle, sticks, some bricks, paper and bottles. Miss Anna Lee is not a bit concerned about how her house looks underneath it. She likes to sit right down on her porch floor in her red checked sleeveless summer dress with wide pockets where she keeps her house keys, her Lucky Strike cigarettes and a book of matches. She lights up one as soon as she puts one out. She takes a puff and coughs two or three times before blowing out the smoke. She swings her legs over the edge like two dangling chicken drumsticks as she chats across the street to my mama or a walker passing by about the sky and the weather "it looks like rain" or it's going to be as hot tomorrow as it is today." Miss Anna Lee reminds me of an Indian squaw we read about carrying on a powwow.

Mrs. Burla's porch is up the street from Miss Anna Lee and across from Mama Allie's. She comes over to sit out with Grandma; they mostly gossip about who said what, what the white man "gone do," the cost of groceries, the cost of coal and oil.

Mama sure does make this time so special with her story telling in the evening if it's raining outside and we can't go for an evening walk or sky watch. Unlike Uncle Horace who tells stories about some animal, some ghost after us to scare us half to death in violence and blood. Mama's stories make us feel good because they have happy endings. When she's telling us a story, her voice rises and falls with the details of the tale and her smile is warm and inviting as she takes her time to indulge in the process.

My two favorite stories are *Rapunzel,* a teen who spent her life in a tower but wanted to see the world. (She reminds me of myself wanting to see the world someday), *The Old Lady Who Couldn't Get Home.* I love the part when Mama says; "The rat begins to gnaw the rope. The rope begins to hang the butcher. The butcher begins to kill the ox; The ox begins to drink the water; The water begins to put out the fire; The fire begins to burn the stick; The stick begins to beat the dog; The dog begins to bite the pig, and the pig jumps over the fence, and the old lady got home that night." I can tell that this is one of Mama's favorites too because she makes it sound like music. She sways her head from side to side with the rhythms of the story, and sometimes she clicks her tongue like the beat of a drum for pauses.

I wake up early; I can hear the birds tweeting outside my window and the sun shines brightly. I dress in my favorite green and red skirt then put on my shoes with my big toe sticking out of the side of the right one, so Mama will give me money for shoes. May is also special because it's my birthday today. I don't know how a twelve year old is suppose to act or look except that everyone of my friends at school and all of the family keep asking me when do I plan to grow. I sure will be glad when they stop asking since I don't have the answer. I'll probably never be big like my sister who folks say, 'grew quickly, womanly, full of life and mischief.' I don't care because they all say I'm pretty. I know old Jimmy is going to try and give me twelve licks at school today. I wish it wasn't a school day so I could stay home and do something fun with Mama like take the local train up to Charlotte to Belks like Vettie. We were usually together on my birthday, but I haven't seen her in weeks. Her house is all locked up now since her father died. Around here they say her family is planning to sell the house and move away. They didn't say where. And I can't ask Vettie because she's not here.

Mama is up and standing at the kitchen sink looking out of the window. She seems to be enjoying the sun, the birds and the morning air. She turns around to speak to me when she hears me come into the kitchen. I sit down at the table waiting for her to say something about my birthday. Last year when I turned eleven, Mama baked my favorite chocolate cake with chocolate icing on top. She usually bakes everyone a cake every year and we sing happy birthday to the birthday person.

I really like the cake completed with icing and all, but I like to eat some while it's still warm before it's been iced as Mama says. Her two-egg cake is the best kind to eat straight from the oven while it's cooling.

"Good morning Emilee, happy birthday!" Mama sure can be some kind of nice when she wants to be. And she sure does know how to make a person feel real good too.

I say, "Thank you Mama." And I go over to the stove to get some breakfast. I get a plate from the sink and dip up some grits, put some butter on them sit down at the table again, bless the food and start to eat.

"What do you want for your birthday?" Mama stands there smiling widely at me, like a brown Genie ready to grant all of my birthday wishes.

"I don't know." I tell her. But secretly in my mind, I wish I had money to eat in the cafeteria everyday with my schoolmates.

"How would you like some money to buy a new pair of shoes from downtown?" She reaches into her dress pocket and pulls out two one-dollar bills and a nickel for taxes that she hands over to me.

"Okay." I say, and reach for the money, take it and lay it on the table beside my plate. I think, if I didn't need shoes, I could use the money for lunch. It only cost twenty cents to eat, so I could eat, let's see, ten days. But my shoe has a hole on the side, and I really do need new ones.

"You and your sister can walk downtown today to Lee's Shoe Store."

"You mean you're going to let Ruth and me walk over the bridge to downtown? I know the way all by myself because we've walked that way a thousand times or more, Mama. Ruth doesn't have to go with me if she doesn't want to." I continue to try to convince Mama, "All I have to do is walk up Blyer Street to Winchester Avenue, go over the bridge to Church Street and Lee's Shoes is right across there on Main."

"Emilee, I've already told Ruth to come straight home from school today so she can go with you." Mama talks like she really wants Ruth and me to go together. "She's got some money from her little job down yonder at the hospital, and she might buy you something from Woolworth's too."

I start thinking about those delicious little chocolate fudge squares with nuts in them that I can buy at JW Woolworth. I sure would like to have some. I think what would be better still, is if we could go to Six Point and have a hamburger, a Coke and a banana split or an ice cream sundae. But we can't sit and eat at the counter like the white people can. We have to get stuff like that at the back door, or we have to eat at Mr. Hersey's place on Winchester Avenue.

I thought the school day would never end. And I didn't see Ruth all day, so I couldn't ask her what time she wanted to leave to go downtown. I rush home as fast as I can and wash up and get ready. I'm in the back room when I hear, "You ready to go, Emilee?" I can see her standing on the front porch. Her voice seems to be filled with the same excitement that I feel. "Come on, girl, let's go." Ruth calls again, only this time louder.

I look for the Vaseline jar to grease my legs, and it's empty so I get some lard and grease my legs real good until they look shiny. I pick up the little pocket book I got for Easter with my two dollars and five cents in it and hurry out to the porch to where Ruth sits waiting on me. I feel like this is the best day in my life. "I'm ready." I say as I stand here at attention.

Ruth looks me over from my head to my feet. She can't help but see this one big toe sticking out of the hole on the side of my shoe. She's inspecting me like she inspects the plates of food before they leave the kitchen before the nurses take the meal to the patients' rooms at the hospital where she works. She reminds me of Mama though. I can't remember a time when she didn't welcome an opportunity to act grown. I wonder how it might be when she's a real adult. With all that the grown people have to worry about, I think she ought to take her time with this growing up thing.

Seems to me it must be awfully tiring. So today I suppose she's having the time of her life being responsible for me.

As we walk, the town is calm and peaceful. Mostly the sounds that we hear are my shoes and Ruth's shoes clanking over the bridge. We get to the end of the bridge and we see Christine wearing a pink and yellow dress standing on the corner of Haynes and Jefferson Street smiling and waving her hand real high and fast. Ruth's feet starts to move faster and I step faster to keep up with her. I can tell that Ruth is glad to see her. And believe it or not, and it's hard for me to figure out, I'm glad to see that Christine is here too. I kind of wish Vettie was here with the three of us.

"Hey girl, whatta you doing down here? I thought you were supposed to be going somewhere with your mom today." Ruth questioned.

"I am. I saw you coming this way so I thought I'd come and wave. Mother is across the street at Secrets Drug store; she had to pick up something before dropping me off at Miss Brewster's for my piano lessons." She motioned with her head toward the drugstore instead of pointing. Then she turns to me, "Hey Emilee. So you're twelve years old today? Happy birthday!" She smiles showing joy in her eyes.

Christine is two and a half years older than Ruth; she's sixteen and she and Ruth started to become best friends when Ruth was skipped a grade ahead in school. It's funny, but usually when these two are together, I get the feeling that I need to make myself scarce or disappear or something. But I don't feel that way today. I give Christine a half smile and a semi-adult look when I put my finger up to the side of my mouth and raise my chin upward like Ruth does, so they might think I'm cool. I wouldn't want her to think I'm a little girl, and I certainly don't want her to think that I'm unsophisticated. We learned all about sophisticated and unsophisticated when we studied the 's' words. And Ruth and Christine can act like the smoothest girls that I know. My sister puts her head in the air like a giraffe floating above all small things in her path. She glides around like nothing can touch her and they have a special look and language code. When she and Christine are together, they put their heads together and laugh at the oddest things. They don't make fun of people, but if they see something or someone strange, they glimpse at each other in a certain way. They sometimes speak with their eyes.

Row 1: The late Rosa Parks and Connie Williams at
Robert F. Williams' eulogy, 1996. The late Mabel

Williams, wife of Robert F. Williams, with Connie Williams. Row 2: The Williams' Family Reunion. Row 3: Connie Williams with her and grandsons Demetrius and Clint Jr.

15

Every morning, now, when I wake up, I try to remember that I have made up my mind to try to keep my life straight because I expect good things to happen instead of worrying about bad ones—what I'm not supposed to do.

My new shoes help to keep me happy. And that bag of a dozen chocolate squares Ruth bought me at Woolworth, the ones I love with the nuts that are much better than sweet water. I eat one every afternoon after school. I'm down to seven, so I'll need to think of another reason to go downtown with Ruth.

I hid them in the corner of my chifforobe draw so Daniel won't find them. I'm surprised he wasn't somewhere looking when I put them there. Thank goodness he has more to occupy his mind these days than to be curious about what I'm doing now that Daddy allowed him to join the Little League Baseball team.

I'm not sure if Mama would say if this is superstition or not, but I can't help feeling that Daddy Claude must be up there in heaven somewhere in the clouds smiling down on me and helping to keep me safe. I sure do hate he's gone. It would be good to have him around when I'm grown and out of school and all or whenever I get lonely, just to have him come and sit on the front porch. Even Witch and Old Woman seem to be different—not causing me fear whenever I pass them in Mama Allie's dining room—maybe because I'm not a little girl anymore.

People need to learn to stand on their own two feet. At least this is what Mama says. So his leaving me worked out for the best because I think situations through. For example, Daniel didn't know it at the time, but his digging up those socks worked out for the best too—it brought my secret out of me. I now feel like a free bird. I feel like my cousin, RW, when he was asked once by a reporter what he wanted, he said, "I just want to be free."

After all everything that happened has caused my sister, my mama and me to be closer than we ever were in our entire lives. Seems like my sister is grinning at me all the time now, and I'm grinning back at her too, like two little lovesick puppies—the taste in my mouth *is* sweet water.

The other day Ruth's best friend, Christine, gave an after school party. I mean a party for **sixteen year olds and I just turned twelve**. Well, as it turned out, my sister invited me to go with her to the party. At first, I was excited and without hesitation chose to go; then later I wasn't sure this was something I should do. Her friends might think I'm tagging along. Besides, a part of me was afraid I might do something silly and childish, since I'm not sure how a twelve year old should act. I guess a part of my mind is still eleven years old trying to jump to thirteen, more grown up, with twelve in the middle. Then, I remembered Ruth's words: *You're a little woman now*.

I suddenly realized that because I'm no longer a baby and should stick with decisions I make. And just maybe Ruth needs me at the party to support her. After all she is closer to my age since I've had a birthday. We are just one year and a half apart; she won't turn fourteen until the fall.

At the party, even Christine treated me real nice. They made sure I had a big slice of coconut cake, which happens to be my absolute favorite cake besides chocolate with chocolate icing on top. I ate two big slices.

I can remember when I wasn't happy about my sister having Christine for her best friend, but if it hadn't been for her, I wouldn't have met her cousin, William who is thirteen years old and just happened to come by who looks better than James with the dimples. And now *I've decided* he's the secret **LOVE** of my life. He smiled at me the entire time while I ate coconut cake.

William said he is a Catholic and belongs to the Catholic Church on Winchester Avenue where Daniel and I went to Vacation Bible School last summer. He said his family was on vacation at Myrtle Beach last summer. I suppose that's the reason we didn't meet then. I told him that I learned the Hail Mary and all while I was there and that Father Robert put me in charge of the game called Spud.

I suppose William was surprised to know that I knew about the Catholic religion and all, being a Baptist myself. I think he was surprised to find out that I could speak French too. I told him all about learning the Lord's Prayer in French when I was two years old. Well, I don't think he was too sure about my knowing it because he made the mistake of asking "How does it go? Why don't you say it then?"

I started out, "Notre Pere qui es aux cieux"... I showed off with it. When I finished, his mouth fell open and I could see his nostrils spread. He blinked and said, "Wow!"

I never turn down an opportunity to show off my French to anyone. But now that I think about it though, I shouldn't have showed off like that. I'm trying to change my ways—including calling Ruth "Archibald", that awful name. I have to keep reminding myself that a part of me still acts eleven, no matter how hard I try not to.

Anyway, Christine came over twice to check on us at the party. She said to see if we wanted anything like punch or cookies or Coke. One more bite of anything and I would have popped. William told Christine that he wanted some punch. She left us and then returned with some red punch in a paper cup and handed it to William. He drank it down quickly and squashed the cup with his hands, and started to throw it high into the air like a ball and catch it.

William stayed and we talked while he kept tossing the crumpled cup into the air for a long time.

Then the strangest thing happened, in a sudden instant. The cup was in the air out of his reach. He stretched to catch it and lost his balance and fell off the porch onto the ground. There was a loud crack and William couldn't move. He couldn't get up. He tried again and again, and he fell down again each time. At first it looked like he was playing with me. Then in an attempt to pull himself up by the bottom step, he gave out a quiet yell—"Ouch!" I knew then that he wasn't playing.

"What's the matter?" I asked him as I ran down the steps where he lay on the ground. "Can't you move—stand up?" I stood over him. William's ankle was twisted. He had fallen on it. He wasn't moving and he began to look like he was in some kind of bad pain.

"Help!" Was all I could shout, "Help!" Was the only thing my brain could think of. I ran up the five porch steps before my mind could catch up with the speed of my feet.

Ruth and Christine were running to the door when I made it to the porch. They passed me and ran to William. When they saw him on the ground, they removed William's shoe and his foot and ankle were swollen and turning sort of blue.

"It's broken. I believe it's broken!" Christine told Ruth, "Go and tell! She yelled. And in a flash, William was rushed away in his mama's white Cadillac to Union Memorial Hospital.

Of all things, believe it or not, once William was better, in the weeks that followed, everyone wanted to tease me. My sister teased me about being so pretty that I cast a spell over William and caused him to lose his balance, fall and break his ankle. Mama even got in on the act and just about laughed her head off. All three of us had a good time talking about poor William that way.

It doesn't take long for any little piece of news to travel around Morris Town. People sit around on their front porches just waiting for something to happen that they can "sink" their teeth into and "chew the fat" as Mama says because everything gets told.

Old Uncle Horace said, "Christine's cousin fell in love so hard that he fell off the porch. He didn't have *no* business trying to dive off the porch to impress me no how."

It's cool that Uncle Horace is still around to tease me, and didn't have to go to the chain gang after all. I was so scared he might have to go to that horrible place.

Mama said "Mama Allie used the money from Daddy Claude's insurance policy to hire a sharp attorney from downtown to keep him out of jail for 'allegedly' shooting out the railroad station lights, and for crawling out of the sheriff's car." Mama said, "The lawyer told the judge, 'Mrs. Allie's son is a hard working, family man; and a proud United States World

War II Army veteran, and he did not deserve to be locked up. When he got himself out of the sheriff's car, he wasn't attempting to escape. He believed he was trying to save his own life. He was afraid he might get harmed by the racist inmates or lynched by one of the hooded men who might come and take him out of jail in the middle of the night. Being in jail is a dangerous experience during these times.'" She said his lawyer further said, "They couldn't prove Horace Allie shot out the lights; there were no witnesses, and Horace said he didn't do it, and he needed to be at home with his wife Glenice and his four children.'" The judge put him on probation, and fined him, Mama said, "A bunch of money." I had to look "probation" up in the dictionary, so I will know what Uncle Horace has to do.

I still haven't figured out how Uncle Horace landed in the yard behind the wash pot after the sheriff picked him up. I supposed if Uncle Horace escaped fox holes with dead bodies while he was in the Army, he could somehow get out of a handcuff and a sheriff's car too, especially when he felt he could get killed. He may not ever explain it to me, but I really, really thought he would be safe once I prayed and called for help.

My uncle might be able to fool the lawyer about needing to be home with his wife Glenice and his children, but he doesn't fool me for one little minute. Uncle Horace is a working man and he's slicker than slick too. As soon as his probation is over, I believe he'll be right back to his old habits, drinking Seagram's Seven, riding that motorcycle, cussin', swearing, grinning and staying out all hours of the night, as Mama Allie says, in juke joints across town because he loves a good time. I believe that's why Ruth can't wait to be grown, so she can hurry up and do some of that same stuff too, maybe with Uncle Horace.

Seems like the story about William falling in love will continue to grow and other people might add their own ending to it until it gets to be real big. Miss Anna Lee took a puff off her cigarette, coughed three times and said, "It just might even end up in the Morris Town Newspaper." Then she pushed the ashes off her cigarette with her finger and took another puff as she sat on her porch swinging her two short legs.

Now that I've gotten the reputation of being so beautiful that boys fall down trying to impress me and all, maybe going to the sixth grade might be fun. Ruth will be in the tenth grade, which won't be bad either now that we're so close and all. I sure am glad she didn't find out what I told Mama about her and Jude kissing and smoking on the back porch. If she found out we would be right back to enemies.

When I look in the mirror these days, I'm sort of starting to kind of look more like her and my mama each day. It seems that I do have Ruth's eyes, and long eye-lashes and Mama's full lips—I suddenly realize I don't look like Aunt Florence *at all*. I look like my mama and my sister *and* my daddy.

I do feel different at age twelve. I've decided and Witch and Old Woman must have decided too that I'm too old for them to scare me now. I just see them as my special friends. When Mrs. Isenhour saved me, I *believe* they must have led her there. I know she travels those parts, being a preacher's wife and all, but she just couldn't have been on the same Roosevelt Boulevard the same time I needed help unless Witch and Old Woman whispered in her ear—telling her where to find me. I *do* believe Miss Mae Lee's cat, the one that disappeared turned into a man with one of his nine lives, because it's mighty strange that Aunt Florence's knight in shining armor showed up and knocked on Mama Allie's door, and introduced himself as a cousin to James, Uncle Horace's brother-in-law. He asked to take my aunt to the movies. Aunt Florence didn't have much to do to prepare herself, because her hair is always curled and her lips are always painted with red lipstick.

Today is Saturday; those crazy Ku Klux Klansmen from Jim Crow don't bother us anymore; while I'm sitting on the porch, a big moving truck passes by and turns down Second Street and pulls into the yard of the second house. Mama said that Mama Allie said that Mrs. Burla told her that Miss Anna Lee said a preacher, his wife, and daughter, who's going to be in the sixth grade, are moving here from Wadesboro. Now that Vettie's family has moved away, maybe the new girl and I will get to be close friends. I look across the yard; the grass is swarming with metallic green phyllophaga beetles. It's funny though. I don't get the urge to play with one anymore—tie a string around the leg and sling it around so it flies like a fan. I'm too **grown up** for that.

The biggest surprise to me now is how Mama and I get along. I'm still not completely sure if I can totally dismiss this superstitious stuff, and I won't be acting like it doesn't mean anything either. If it's important to Mama, then it's surely important to me. And that's all there is to that.

****

After supper, Daddy said, "Martha why don't we go over to Bent Hill, to hear Papa preach tomorrow and eat dinner at the big house?" Daddy has to pose it diplomatically, as a question, to get Mama to think she has made the decision. So she agreed. Well, it seems I can look forward to seeing my cousin Barbara this weekend on Bent Hill at Papa Will's. I'll get a chance to tell Barbara all about William, the secret *LOVE* of my life.

Epilogue

In the late nineteen fifties when the country was becoming aware of my cousin, Robert F. Williams, the local NAACP President, and Civil Rights activist, Williams announced in the *Monroe Enquirer*, "All citizens who believe in democracy, the rights of man, and brotherhood are urged to join and support the NAACP. This organization is open to all people, irrespective of race, who support the American cause as embodied in the United States Constitution."

When Mr. Williams made his announcement in the *Monroe Enquirer*, I had just embarked upon the beginning of my teenage years.

Emilee, a pre-teen and our protagonist in this story, ***Green***, could not have fully understood, at such a young age, the magnitude of the civil rights struggle for blacks in the South, and in her environment. I have written the novel, ***Green***, because there is a need for stories to be told from the young female perspective of the tumultuous civil rights era for our readers.

It wasn't until I was a student, living on the west coast, and matriculating at California State University at Northridge in the mid 70s, when I became a part of the camaraderie of the Black Students' Union that was partly organized by Professor W. Burwell, that I discovered the book Robert F. Williams had written, entitled, ***Negroes with Guns***.

When I returned to North Carolina in the late 70s, and began a school teaching career, I also began to take writing seriously. I therefore, took an enduring interest in the life of Robert F. Williams, firstly, because I had read his book in college, so I knew he was an important man with a commitment to freedom, justice and civil rights; secondly, because I was a member of the "kinfolk" at our family reunions where we intermingled with all the members and exchanged ideas with him, his wife Mabel, his son Reverend John Williams, and his brother John Herman Williams, and lastly, because I honored him and was in awe with what he stood for - equality, and self-respect, self-determination. He was a man who overcame overwhelming obstacles in life in his brave fight for social justice for the common man. After all, he escaped becoming lynched, a brilliant and miraculous feat, during the Jim Crow racist era of the South in the 60s. I could identify with him so much, because, I myself, overcame so many obstacles in life (saving *my* own life at a young age and educating my mind) to advance to where I am today, now writing this novel. However, although *I* suffered risk and dangers, my experiences do not parallel Mr. Williams' encounters.

At one family reunion in 1984, I had the privilege and pleasure of interviewing Robert F. Williams, who spoke honestly and candidly about some of his life experiences as the president of the NAACP in Monroe, North Carolina and living abroad in Cuba and China.

During my teaching career, 1979-2014, I researched and collected a great amount of provocative materials about Mr. Williams. In 2012 I proposed an idea to the "Lynching without Sanctuary" Conference committee at the University of North Carolina at Charlotte, where I taught English Communication. My proposal was accepted. In completing this research, I consulted with Reverend John Williams, son of Robert F. Williams, who instantaneously gave me his blessings and approval. He continued, effortlessly, to communicate with me until the research was completed.

In the summer of 2012, I wrote *Story of a Hero (Robert F. Williams) and Anti-Lynching*, a chronology of violent, racial events and experiences surrounding Mr. Williams' life in his fight for justice and dignity: the violence leveled against Blacks during the 50s and 60s by the Ku Klux Klan, and the race riot in Monroe in the 60s, the phony kidnapping charge, the FBI dragnet he escaped, going into exile with his family into Canada, Cuba and finally China, up until the exoneration of all charges against him in 1969, his return to the United States, and his passing away in the safety of his own home in1996.

My work, *Story of a Hero (Robert F. Williams) and Anti-Lynching* was presented at the University of North Carolina, Center City, at the "Lynching Without Sanctuary" Conference, October, 2012 to a full, diverse audience and distinguished presenters from universities and organizations from around the globe.

During the year of the race riot in Monroe (referred to as Morris Town in the novel) I was living in either, Monroe, Washington, DC or Brooklyn, New York and returning to my hometown for short intervals. My ten siblings, as youngsters did experience the episodic and violent upheaval.

The following is a researched account of some of the events based on actual occurrences; some accounts are referred to in the story **GREEN** as our character

Emilee watched TV with her parents, Jomis and Martha, and her siblings, Ruth and Daniel:

The reporter says, "Whites chased RW and a carload of Negroes down the highway after they and some Freedom Riders picketed the "whites only" swimming pool, and when their car was finally forced off the road and came to a stop, white men carrying guns surrounded it. RW and his followers jumped out of his car unexpectedly with their guns, and suddenly gunshots were exchanged, which made the Whites run away in fear for their own safety. One white man fell to the ground and cried. "The 'GD' niggers have got guns, and the police can't even arrest them. Oh Lord, oh Lord; what has this world come to!"

Later on in Bright Town, a riot developed; gun warfare of black and white citizens and the police outbreak in front of the courthouse square and in Bright Town sent some blacks running for their lives after being shot at by white men wearing police uniforms. This went on downtown, on the railroad tracks, and the streets.

Demonstrators were shot, imprisoned without medical attention. Once in jail, they were brutally beaten by white cellmates, receiving broken ribs and severe head injuries.

A white rampage combed through the black community. RW supporters armed themselves with shotguns, semiautomatic military carbines and went downtown to try to save the picketers, where they were met with armed guns pointing and firing at them. A horrible gun battle caused a police officer to get hit with a bullet in his thigh. The black men had to run back to Bright Town on foot.

Carloads of Klan racists roamed through the city all night, attacking blacks and some whites they called liberal whites. The Klan shot through houses. The Bright Town Journal article said, "A bloody racial war went on. Black people in droves ran to Bright Town, barely escaping mob-hooded white attackers."

Hundreds of blacks formed at RW's house in Bright Town, many of them armed. They feared the jailed people would not survive the night.

Some angry blacks talked of killing white people. RW's aim was to settle the crowd and keep them from danger. Controlling the battered and frightened citizens was extremely challenging, however, as members of the NAACP, they finally responded to RW in a disciplined and organized manner.

It was necessary to barricade certain streets, mainly Tobye Street, posting young followers who positioned themselves in trees along Winchester Avenue. Young men stood guard with guns on porches. They set up effective defense perimeters.

Speaking calmly with authority, RW told black men, "If the Klan rides and tries to do wrong against you, stop them, protect your family, and your home. The weapons are not for killing. Killing is wrong."

The outbreak of violence prompted state troopers. Governor Terry Sanford's office intervened, but had to keep a safe distance from RW's barricaded perimeters and keep the whites from there. News of violence spread to other parts of the country. People were calling from the county and the country about their sons and daughters. RW, who had formed allies around the county and the country, was constantly on the telephone.

While RW was on the telephone, later that evening two white citizens, known for advocating separatism, accidently drove into the angry crowds. Their car was surrounded, and they were pulled out. The couple later reported being surrounded by "niggers."

RW heard the unrest in the streets and came out, taking the couple into his home for safety against the angry wishes of the agitated crowd. His personal intervention prevented any violence against them, and he reprimanded anyone who desired causing harm to the couple. The couple was lodged until later that night when they could leave the neighborhood safely.

The police and the FBI charged RW with allegedly kidnapping of the couple. The federal and state government issued an FBI Most Wanted warrant, citing RW as **Armed and Extremely Dangerous.**

The main concern was the fate of the innocent protesters, who were still behind bars in the downtown jail. That night the police chief called RW and promised to send state troopers. He also promised RW, "**In thirty minutes you'll be hanging in the court house square.**"

At that point RW realized the limitations of his armed strategies under the circumstances of the Jim Crow law of the South.

With little hope of any understanding from the justice system, RW made a decision to avoid being lynched. That night, he and his family mysteriously escaped from Bright Town into New York, Canada and Cuba. They later lived in China under Mao Zedong. RW later reported, "If I had not escaped from Bright Town, there would have been a blood bath."

Once told by the police, "Your father was a good man and never gave us any trouble." RW responded, "That's why I have to." The trouble he spoke about concerned black pride, human rights and justice, supposedly guaranteed by the US Constitution—the right to life, liberty and the pursuit of happiness-human rights that were being denied to black citizens. RW went on to say, "The most trouble you can get into is to try and see that the Constitution applies to all humanity."

A charismatic and powerful leader left an ineffaceable mark on the Morris Town consciousness and the world. He also stated to me in the 1984 interview, "I'm reminded of the five hundred or so FBIs chasing me with their dogs as I escaped from Monroe into Canada to avoid the promise of Mauney, the Monroe police chief, to lynch me. The image of the sled dog Husky and the Royal Canadian Mounted Police were in my mind because of what they represented. The television newsreel of the dogs that showed before the actual featured film in the 60s had as its motto, '**We**

always get our man. I didn't want the white man to get me, as they did Malcolm and Martin, for loving their country and their freedom. Kennedy loved his country, yet he went on to become the president. Our black men are killed for that. I wanted to die in the quietness of my own home—in my own bed."

In 1969, RW (Robert F. Williams) was cleared of all charges stemming from the alleged kidnapping in Monroe.

I was well into adulthood in 1996 when RW (Robert Franklin Williams, Sr.) was eulogized in my hometown, his birthplace in Monroe, NC. It was said by Mrs. Rosa Parks, who spoke so eloquently at his memorial, which I, along with hundreds of family members and worldly figures attended, "Mr. Williams could have been a rich and famous man, but he chose to dedicate his life to the 'good fight' for justice and equality for his oppressed brothers and sisters. His name should go down in history and never be forgotten."

Acknowledgments

This book is a work of the mind's eye, but a number of sources have proved noteworthy, including:

Banchero, S. "Hero Or Renegade?." *The Charlotte Observer*. Feb. 1995.

Catterall, B. "Is it all coming together?" Robert F. Williams. V 10 No. 1 2006.

Como, P. "The Lord's Prayer Lyrics." Networks.

Haley, A. *The Autobiography of Malcolm X*. NY: Grove Press, 1964.

Handkerchief:https://www.youtube.com/watch?v=xcAB kW7 wNgs

James, B. "Friends Organizing Monroe Homecoming." *The Charlotte Observer*. Mar. 1995.

Leiber, Jerry and Mike Stoller. "Kansas City." 1952

Obama, B. *Dreams from My Father*, NY: Three Rivers

Press, 1995

Photographs page 206: From top to bottom: Row 1:

Ms.   Rosa Parks and Connie Williams.   Mabel

Williams, late wife of the late Robert Williams

and Connie   Williams. Row 2: Williams' family

reunion. Row 3: Connie Williams and grandsons,

Demetrius   and Clint Jr.

Parks, Rosa, Testimony and Remarks, *Homegoing*

Celebration for Mr. Robert Franklin

Franklin Williams, Sr. NC: Oct. 1996.

Potter, Timothy, "A Couple of Years before His

Time, RFW." NC: Nov. 2003.

Shropshire, Louise. "We Shall Overcome." 1955.

Williams, Connie. Personal interview: R. Williams

during a family reunion. 3 July, 1984.

Williams, R.F. *Negros With Guns.* Ill: Third World Press,

1972.

Workers World Newspaper. NY: Nov. 21, 1996.

About the Author

Connie Williams was born in Union County, North Carolina the second of eleven children to the late Jones and Lillie Williams upholstery business owners, who were vital to the community, and before their passing away in '10 and '11 celebrated their 68th wedding anniversary. Williams' first novel, **Emily's Blues**, a self-published collaboration with the International Black Writers of Charlotte and L&S Printing, '89 was carried in libraries and major bookstores and widely read.
She was awarded the Arts and Science Council Emerging Artist Grant for this work in 1990.

Her stage play, "Emily's Dilemma" '90, was funded by the Union County Community Arts Council for five years for her educational arts program: The Emily's Blues Self-Actualization Project; it was awarded the Honorable Terry Sanford Local Award for Creativity, Honorable

Mention. Her play was performed at Piedmont High School in Union County and Livingstone College at Salisbury, North Carolina by her students.

Novello Festival Press published her short story and recipe, "Mama Allie's Talking Dogs Fried Croakers in Peanut Oil", '03 in **Hungry for Home,** Rogers.

She taught high school English in her home town '84-'96 received her M. Ed at the University of North Carolina at Charlotte, '88; transferred to Charlotte Mecklenburg Schools, where she simultaneously taught English at Garinger High School and UNC at Charlotte 1996-2014. (She retired from CMS '06; retired from UNCC '14).

The ideas for **Green**, however, began during her Fellowship at Headlands Center for the Arts, Sausalito, California. The Headlands Fellowship was generously funded by a grant from the North Carolina Arts Council and the National Endowment for the Arts.

Williams is the mother of four daughters, a grandmother and great grandmother. She resides in Charlotte with her husband. She is currently completing a fourth literary work (an inspirational testimony); a children's book; a researched prose work, and a book of poetry.